PETER

OWEN

A PETER OW

CW00521010

When the Whip Comes Down

By the same author

Fiction

Inhabiting Shadows
Isidore
Delirium

Non-Fiction

Madness – The Price of Poetry
Lipstick, Sex and Poetry (autobiography)

Poetry

Nineties

Jeremy Reed

When the Whip Comes Down

A Novel about de Sade

Peter Owen
London & Chester Springs

PETER OWEN PUBLISHERS
73 Kenway Road London SW5 0RE
Peter Owen books are distributed in the USA by
Dufour Editions Inc. Chester Springs PA 19425–0449

First published in Great Britain 1992
© Jeremy Reed 1992

All Rights Reserved.
No part of this publication may be reproduced in any form
or by any means without the written permission of the
publishers.

A catalogue record for this book is
available from the British Library

ISBN 0 7206 0857 0 (hardback)
0 7206 0858 9 (paperback)

Printed in Great Britain by Billings of Worcester

We, too, we know how to create.

D.A.F de Sade

Mine is the poverty of angels, I just don't give a damn about possessions and the like. . . . I write, and that's enough. Most of our activities have the vagueness and vacantness of a tramp's existence. We very rarely make a conscious effort to transcend that state. I transcend it by writing.

Jean Genet

Introduction

Much maligned, misconstrued, and I suspect little read, the
Marquis de Sade has become a name on which to hang
sexual preferences, a figure evoked for the purposes of
psychopathology, and insufficiently considered as a man,
a revolutionary, an ideological nihilist whose private
torment is reflected in the obsessive erotomania of his
fiction.

My novel is not an attempt to telescope de Sade into
historic fact and chronology. What we have come to inherit
from him is the realization that his propensities are inherent
in all of us, and that archetypal patterns of behaviour are
fluent. The ethos in which we live is the psyche. The de
Sade I have created for the purposes of this novel is one
who vitalizes the immediate, one who is equally at home in
the foundations of a recollected life involving crime and
imprisonment, as he is now, inhabiting an imaginary
La Coste, returning there each autumn to resume his sexual
dialogue with a number of chosen initiates.

The time-leap involved in this transposition of de Sade
from a prisoner at the Bastille or an inmate at Charenton to
a man still alive at the end of the twentieth century is a
plausibly imaginative one. The protagonist of my book has
watched over the centuries, he has entered a deathless state,
he has discovered the secret of DNA and an indestructible
life-force, he is now and always.

The historical novel *per se* doesn't interest me. De Sade, who wished to break the constraints of his age, would hardly have wished to be returned to a particular code of moral ethics. Biography can reconstruct his life to some degree. My aim has been to extend his potential, wire his nerves to the excitement of our crazy, fragmented times. I have not wished the menace of his person to be a thing of the past; I have intended to programme his nerve-impulses to the present.

My novels have invariably invited controversy. Re-creating a character from lyric spontaneity rather than from accepted fact leaves one open to the whiplash of critics conditioned to a fiction of social realism, with the inevitable clichéd dialogue that the latter implies. Limitations are what de Sade hated; animals in cages resent captivity, and so does the imagination.

We can restructure history, but we can't inhabit it authentically. We can empathize with what it was like for de Sade, an aberrant and impoverished aristocrat, to find himself repeatedly imprisoned for sodomy, to suffer ignominy, constraint, and ultimately insanity, but we're inhabitants of a very different knowledge and sensibility to those who dictated the political, philosophic, religious and social thinking of his age.

My challenge has been to invest de Sade with a psychological continuity. It is arguably in the novels of Genet, Burroughs and Ballard that de Sade's sexual proclivities are reconstituted. He is translated into the gene-pool of a fiction that risks extremes. By giving play to the autonomy of his unconscious, by uncompromisingly voicing the inner reality of erotic fetishism, the turbulence of his mind has intersected with the atrocities of twentieth-century warfare, the collective S&M cults which characterize our millennial decade.

As individuals we resist classification into specific types. De Sade was conscious of inventing himself in the way that we all inhabit fictional selves. There are lots of empty rooms in the mind, we may choose to use each for a different function. And the interior of one may incorporate the design of de Sade's bedroom at La Coste, rumoured to be panelled with erotic frescoes, the central scene depicting someone receiving an enema. Other spaces will be blank, white or blue. Most are occupied by images, subjective fantasies, and de Sade applied a lion-tamer's concentration to dominating the menagerie of orgiastic subjects who streamed through his unconscious before finding embodiment on the page.

When I write, my concern is with the new, the unbalancing of the status quo. Why bother to create if one merely repeats the past or settles for accepted literary conventions? We need to be shocked out of complacency, and de Sade is the best antidote to the state of feeling comfortable.

And time? We can be here or anywhere in the imagination. My distinctly modern creation is in orbit: a de Sade who is still arriving, one who is constantly being modified by our understanding of sexual modalities. I hope as you are driving, his Mercedes is in your rear-view mirror. The Marquis may catch up with you yet.

Jeremy Reed
1992

One

It begins with an ass. The delectable proportions of a
pumpkin, slit to allow a point of entry. I've never been able to
view women or men in any other manner. They have to be
turned that way round, their genitalia concealed, their faces
hidden before my adrenalin fires and my need asserts itself
through the stimulus of watching and being watched. It's
natural to me. It's the others who are aberrant. They follow
an orthodoxy which demands the trust of face-to-face
contact. It's as though they need to see each other in order to
modulate their passion. I prefer our heads to have no point of
contact. I want to re-create that person through the imagination, and have them conceive of me as they wish. A man, a
mythic beast, a primal incarnation. Someone dressed in
orange silk with a black leather mask over his eyes. Someone
who can never die.

In my early years at the château of Saumane, perched
amongst mauve rocky summits in the Vaucluse, I would
experience an excitement when the dark came down in
winter. What I felt was a settling-in, a deepening of my own
centre, a detachment from others by virtue of my privileged
rank and the controlled mania I delighted in checking,
knowing that one day I would unleash it on the world. Desire
sat in my head like a panther. A black, brooding tornado, its
eyes pretending indifference. But sometimes, when I caught

myself in mid-thought, when I became conscious of the notion of my singular identity, the cat's eye-slits would open full to ferocious green suns. I knew already that my core of rage was indomitable. Everything shrank in obedience to my inner dictates. I had only to subject a person, an imaginary situation, to my autonomous stream of consciousness, to assert a superiority which ended in savagery. I have always despised mediocrity, those who accept in order to conform. They are the custodians of limitation. Their minds are blanked out or flooded like sea-sponges.

It comes back to me. The black satellite, a speck that orbits consciousness, always too far out to register, before it picks up speed to intersect with a moment of ferocity. A black sun smokes into my rage. At four, I threw myself on someone twice my age. I can see it still. The sunlight slanting through a line of breezily skirted poplars, my opponent somehow involved in those shifting, horizontal shadows. It didn't mean anything to me that he was the Prince Louis-Joseph. He was an obstacle. An oval blur, his white face defiant with a self-assumed authority. At that moment I couldn't believe a person might come between me and my intentions. Something snapped. There were colour blotches to my right and left – emerald, cerise, saffron dresses. But the colours didn't belong to people. They might have been voluminous silks given shape by hangers. I was no longer standing in a park illuminated by the late afternoon sun. Instead I was energy overtaking itself. My antagonist seemed immobilized. His was a white moon-face that came too close up for me not to hit. He wouldn't retreat. And the more I lashed out, the more suffocatingly near that face drew. It seemed set up as a static target. There were red zigzags running across the expressionless mask. And suddenly there were violent hands restraining me, the hysteria of women in a background in which the sound seemed abruptly turned on; and most forcibly, someone scooping me up, pulling me back, feet off the ground, to struggle like a fly hung up in gossamer.

I can't stand up in my cell. Two small, heavily barred windows admit chinks of white light. Sometimes I hold out my hands and feel the light weigh in my palms. My lair is recessed behind nineteen iron doors. Just thinking about that becomes an impossibility. I bore a mental hole through each, and then have to project nineteen separate escapes. I would have to thin myself to a snake to make good my exit. Wriggle through each as a serpentine spiral, my fangs needling into my opponent's jugular.

The seasons come and go unnoticed. But I smell, I relive, I internalize experience. Red woods wet with autumn, wines that sat on my palate evoking an entire region, violet chocolates fresh from the window display, crisp linen, the crotchless silk panties of a red-haired prostitute hired unsuspectingly to fulfil my bizarre fetishes. And habitable space. The kick I got from secret rooms kitted out with instruments of correction, and from conducting sex in rooms at La Coste which remained deep and serene as mountain lakes: this is not transferred into the suffocating sack-like confines of a cell in which I have howled like a wolf in the hills.

All this time at Vincennes, and soon they will remove me to the Bastille, and I still write to the wife whom I have disgraced socially. I need an external focus on which to direct and modify my outrage. And also one that serves as a point of memory. What I do, what I have done, is liberated by a stream of black ink. It is the arrowhead for my nerves and blood, the missile advancing into the unpredictable reaches of space.

I can live out the ritual again and again. I used to tie up my auburn hair with a handkerchief, take off my jacket and white shirt and adopt a black leather waistcoat. I would have X lie face down on the bed, and tie her hands to one end and her feet to the other. I would always look for beauty-spots on her bottom, little black islands on a lunar surface. I would complete her bondage by tying a rope round her waist. By that time I was someone else: dissociated, animalized, conscious only of the compacted sexual tension that hummed in my body. And how can I regret an emotion in which pain is more delectable than pleasure? Usually the two are distinct. I experience a reverse of the natural order. It excites me to commit what I acted out in cold rage to the medium of words.

I would use a birch rod to create mauve horizontals on the bottom presented. It was incredible just watching those welts appear, for it heated my desire to have the same done to me. The whistling pliancy of my birch set up a tornado in the room. A dialogue between wood and flesh, a punctuated sibilance which kept me erect. And there are the things said of me. That I made knife incisions and poured red sealing wax into the wounds I had opened in the prostrate girl. And having lacerated that person I demanded that I receive the same with a whip studded with long and short nails. After each lash I would cut the number of strokes given to me into wood with my knife. I wanted no error to counteract my obsession with numbers. The implied, occult meaning of numerology was written into my understanding at birth.

Let me tell you a story. It may be true or false. That's up to you to decide. By the time we read or hear anything we've converted the original into a fiction. We are all stories, some of them good, some of them bad. And me, my narrative is continuous. I am the past become the future.

I was once somebody, by which I mean that I was born to a privileged class which took delight in ruining me once I had fallen. I was out walking. It was night. Heavy rainfall had turned the chestnut trees into chandeliers. Dark foliage was loaded with crystal. I wasn't looking for anything in particular, unless it was the clue to life through the random, ambiguous images that consciousness projects. What I found was a cat. And the cat led me to a door; and the door opened to a person. But it wasn't just that. Should I tell you that the cat was black with yellow eyes? And that the person was neither man nor woman, but someone into whom I could insert without ever knowing their identity. We didn't even speak. I was taken upstairs and shown into a room in which there was nothing but a circular leather bed beneath a mirrored ceiling. Something of my enmity towards both sexes disappeared in this union. It was like making love to a new species.

What a person demands of sex – and the projection is usually from inner to outer, the fantasy being imposed on the partner – is something I rejected. I wanted others to experience visually my pain and orgasmic frenzy, and I wanted to project their longing to be me at the moment of crisis into the body I had hired for this purpose. At the moment of orgasm I was the tornado destroying a coastal town. A hallucinated maelstrom of vengeance tore through me. There was no power comparable to my detonation. And its aftermath was screaming. People attempted to run out of the room, only to find the doors locked. They were brought face to face with what they had seen. They had to learn to let it sink in, go deep and become a reality. And I was already coming out of trance, anxious to be free of the presence of those necessary to my pleasure. I wanted to be alone, striding out under a yellowing oak canopy, or withdrawn into myself, finding the points on the inner map where one can take refuge and be alone. Those are the secret places in which one lives. If I was to look for traces of my existence, it would be there in the journey to the interior.

I was married. I turned my wife into a procuress. Renée-Pélagie. A Montreuil. How could she be expected to know of my duality, the incurable sexual mania which overtook me? There was a nervous fidget in the area beneath her left eye. Unsynchronized nerve-endings that twitched. If I turned up my volume of power and stared at her, I could kill that irregularity.

The things I want arrive or they don't. Linen, suits, perfumes, pastries, vanilla chocolates, paper, ink. And what comes to me seems out of place. It's as though those commodities lost their identity on entering my cell. They revert to their thingness: I can't personalize them. My only way to percolate my rage and to avenge myself for being reduced to a crouched, squint-eyed, partially lobotomized lion in a cell is to write. In that focus I am the still eye in a hurricane. I can subvert the future by my assassination of the present. Writing is the vein that unseams the universe. A good line is like a surgeon's scar which refuses to heal.

If I imagine a castle sealed off from the world in the Black Forest, a place so far removed from human interest that every manner of debauch can go on there unnoticed, then I am in effect opening the furnace door to my unconscious and entering into a space where the ungovernable beast skirts the walls with a speed that removes the skin from its body. The panther is reduced to a mangy cat. Its sores irritate its swinging genitals. When it realizes attraction in another it wants to roar. I have no time for compromise. I lacked it then, and even more so now.

What do the straight, the conformist, the mediocre ever learn of life? If they haven't shifted dimension, then they haven't lived. There are men who suck sherbet from a straw believing it to be cocaine. There are others who devote themselves to the pursuit of money and end up as blind, misshapen horses, put out to grass at the field's far corner. They have to learn all over again that the spiral of incarnation demands that we take experience to the outermost extremes. Delirium is the condition in which we most know ourselves. The pressurized build-up to orgasm is one way of getting there; the ecstatic ballistics take me into an overreach in which I am a projectile blasting through inner space.

Now that there's no immediate way out I can begin to go to the interior. There are always men hurrying about the street on business, while others are making their way inwards. I have known both. I have had food pushed at me through a hole and I have been grateful for it. And after eating I have lain like a snake, bloated, inert, digesting the poison I would in time convert to words. And words are weightless entities while they belong to thought; but commit them to paper and they weigh. The physical labour involved is like pushing the carriages of a freight train across the length of Siberia. It's a long, inexorable journey. Those who die in war, those who tyrannize others from behind an office desk, travel light in comparison. The politician can wave his arms in the air. My hand is tied to the page and the other serves as balance. Writing involves such an odd posture. It appears that the hand is thinking, whereas in truth it is struggling to keep pace with the mind's autonomy. And in time it grows heavy. It becomes like a bird with a broken wing and crumples. Anatomists should examine a writer's hand at death. It's been travelling all its life, always moving right towards the edge. And then it returns on its arc in shadow. There must be a

14

lesson in this. Right to left and back again. It is the creation of a world within the radius of physical limitations.

I'm both constrained and liberated. The man who brings my food has the bestial ebullience of someone whose intolerance suggests he has never forgiven the world for not putting him inside a cage. And I defiantly guard my prerogative. I want to remain here in order to perpetrate atrocities on mankind. At first I resisted confinement. My fingers bled from contact with stone. My voice grew hoarse from shouting, and when I stopped I could still hear myself. What I imagined was not a triumphant release, but a removal to somewhere so remote I need never be disturbed in my solitude. The further you get away from humans, the more extreme are the choices of auto-eroticism, the more vindictive one's imaginings of universal revenge.

What do you the reader know of me? Nothing, except your preconceived idea of de Sade. Was I once a young subaltern, dressed in a royal-blue cloak and uniform with red facings? Was it I who took part in the invading force, crossing the Rhine and striking into the plains of northern Germany? The Hanoverians fumed in the intense June heat. Man and horse were united in a common sweat. And if it was me involved in this bloody Turkish bath, this immobilized ruck of men isolated under a spotlight, then I have long come to disown this fragmented chip of biography. I am someone else.

But something stands out and demands attention from that time. It's like a snap-shot that memory insists on retaking. I was on top of a German girl in the outhouse to a farm. A long shaft of sunlight reddened the straw. I was looking for the kind of gratification which had already come to bore me. The position was one of thrust and counter-thrust. A fox must have got in the previous night for there was a blizzard of threshed feathers just to the right of the entrance. My sex was low-key. When I looked up I could see a horsewhip hanging from a nail in the wall. I let the image hang suspended in my mind. It floated there as a pike might bask in still water, its submarine lethargy concealing a savage voracity. At that moment of repressed orgasm, there seemed to be an irreparable gulf between my imaginings and the girl to whom

15

I was connected. The light was increasing in the barn. The sun must have come out behind clouds, its scarlet streamers diffused through blue and black cumuli. It was suddenly too bright. I felt overexposed, humiliated by this abject lovemaking. One moment I was part of an undulating confluency – a ripple in the erotic current – and the next I was free, I had withdrawn with an abruptness that shocked my blonde-haired partner. Her body was still working in time to my rhythm. She was moving towards a ghost climax. All I knew was that the whip I had sighted was necessary to my balance. Even before I picked it up I knew its weight, its casual flick and assertive lash. The girl hadn't recovered from my absence. Her arms were seeking an intangible body. And suddenly it became very clear to me what I had to do. It was as though my life had been a preparation for this outrage. The red of the setting sun was transferred into a hurricane inside my head. Everything seemed immobile. Time seemed to have stopped. The girl had rolled on to her stomach as though involuntarily anticipating my needs. She was trying to shut out her rejection, and she lay with her head in her hands, directing her crowded thoughts into a singular dark. Something had snapped in me. I could feel the severance, like two wires which had disconnected. I wanted to hurt her for making me pity her. She recoiled at the first crack. She couldn't believe that the blow had fallen on her. And for disbelieving it I struck her again with greater ferocity. And for not offering any form of resistance I let fly again. I could feel the sweat pinking in hot beads from my forehead. I had lost count. I was dripping in a lather of sweat. The girl must have run off at some point for the whip was striking up dust from the bed of straw that I was repeatedly hitting. I was close to fainting. I wanted to turn the instrument on myself, but lacked the facility to have it bite into my flesh in a series of blue- and maroon-coloured welts. There was always this limitation. Just when I tried to overtake myself I was pulled up by the body's shortcomings. I threw the whip into the straw and watched its expended life quiver like a shot snake. The sun had moved on and shadows striped the blond floor. I wanted to lie down and rest, but thought it more expedient to get back to my company. My clothes were soaked with the fury of my sweat. I looked like a horse trainer who had been out bareback riding a recalcitrant stallion. There were deep cuts in my palm. The whip-handle had scarred my flesh. It was my first sadistic stigmata.

Thinking back to that experience from the distance that retrospect affords, I feel my nerves quicken. Electric messages travel the length of my spine. The full white buttocks that I whipped are again tangible in my hands. In my imagination I enter her; she's never had it from behind and flinches at the incompatibility between my size and the narrowness of her passage. She would have to be a train tunnel to accommodate my urgency. And I'm unstoppable. My horizontal wants to stand up vertical. I want to pivot her body on my cock, have it rotate as though a nest of escaped ants tickled my prepuce, sensitize the tip as though it was being licked through a dome of honey.

Some men go into the world to find themselves. They ransack its four quarters. I came here into the retreat of a cell to imagine what I had experienced. At times I'm ursine. I'm reduced to a cave animal in the middle of a civilized city. What do they want of me? Do they assume I have spent my life emulating the sexual licentiousness of the Duc de Richelieu or the Abbé Dubois?

They thought that by imprisoning me they would restrain me. On the contrary I have never been more dangerous. Unable to consummate my pleasures in the world, I have set about a revenge which will shock posterity. The permutations of my sexual interest have I believe superseded those of any individual who has ever given voice to his needs. There is no zone of the body to which I have lacked access. I have known men become women and women adopt the traits of men. And it's in this inversion that pleasure is to be found. Put a person of either gender into their reverse image and the pleasure they derive from unnatural sex is excruciating.

I am who? Donatien-Alphonse-François de Sade. Born of one of the first families of France, propertied at La Coste, at Saumane, at Mazan and Arles. Related to Laura de Sade, who married Hugues de Sade in 1325, and who became the Laura of Petrarch's sonnets. It is she who is the signifier in my dreams; her light dazzles my hallucinated nights.

Let me tell you of the dream in which she came to comfort me. I had been reading Petrarch with an indescribable pleasure and avidity. It was close to midnight. I had fallen asleep with the book in my hand. And suddenly she was there. It wasn't a trick of the light; nothing could impair the brilliance of her standing in my cell. She was dressed in black; her blonde hair floated over her shoulders as though in a slipstream. She said to me in my dream: 'You too can achieve space. I'm dead, but it's not necessary for you to die. Your inner dimension will be realized through physical continuity.'

And why do I feel loyalty to this dead woman? Perhaps it is the little tincture of her that exists in me. And after two years of living like a beast in its own excrement, I can still call to mind the contents of my dream, and how that voice was instrumental in directing my future.

Poetry consoles me; the world fires me to the dangerous pressure we associate with mania. In my confinement I imagine myself walking across great tracts of countryside. It's a wet autumnal day on the road, and shoals of red and yellow leaves flutter across my path. I'm reminded that freedom means the ability to encounter space. In my mind I go on walking in order to think. My feet are wet from the cold proliferation of dew. If I was pulled up and questioned I wouldn't be able to explain where I was going or why. A big red bird fat with blood opens its wings across the fields.

The wines of Meursault, Chablis, the Hermitage, the Loire, Montepulciano are there to flavour the palate. We acquire a taste for them as we do the more subtle orifices of the body. It's a heightened olfactory stimulus that has brought me face to face with a wall whichever way I turn. And if that wall was alternately blue, red, green, violet, would it matter? I've already acquired the habits of a chameleon. If you came into my cell you wouldn't know me from the floor, the walls, the ceiling. You wouldn't be able to discern my presence even though your body would occupy a third of the area of my enclosure. I and it have grown into the one substance: the granite in which Man Ray conceived my face.

I'm stone. I've seen myself in the subsequent Man Ray depictions, his drawing of me with my profile crenellated as though hewn from the walls of the Bastille. Is that me? And his photographic *Monument to de Sade*, in which the convulsively provocative ass is framed within a cross. He has depicted the exact cleavage which incited me to sexual delirium. In that passage I discovered rain-forests, jewelled caves, a black book open on the secrets of the occult universe, orgies enacted on volcanic beaches. The deeper I went the nearer I came to penetrating the mystic eye.

And I've seen others. Allen Jones's *Chair*, in which the doll wears black leather panties, gloves and boots. She has become a chair as the girls do in *Juliette*. And there I am in Clovis Trouille's *Luxure*, a refined aesthete surrounded by the half-dressed girls I am in the process of whipping, all black stockings and high heels, while the ruins of a devastated La Coste serve as the background. And here I am in Hans Bellmer's images *A Sade*, which depict a cannibalistic eroticism, a paroxysmic convulsion in which the figures are anamorphic; glutinous and transgressive, they are in the process of making sex into something involving a finger and a sea anemone.

And here I am in Magritte's *La Philosophie dans le boudoir*. The empty shoes have assumed toes, the dress on the hanger has developed breasts. Do any of these images help me? Did I really contribute to their making? How one life translates into another has to do with the momentum of that state we call empathy. Something of my life, my work, remains as the transmission of a current. Posterity is no more than a series of electric impulses. Anyhow, there have been facts in my life, as much as I dislike them. My army career ended abruptly. By the time the Peace of Paris was negotiated in February 1763 by Louis XV's prime minister, the Duc de Choiseul, I had returned home. And that involves creating a fictitious war for one's listeners. I am still doing that today.

I was already displaced. I wanted the sort of kicks that came about only by moving amongst exclusive circles. I was a leader, a prophet, a blueprinter of a new sexual ethos. Back home some of the scandal that had blown up around my name was dispersed by the hectic objurgation directed at my former guardian the Abbé de Sade. The police had raided a brothel that the Abbé was known to attend, and discovered him in bed with two girls. His pleasures were spiked with the bizarre. He was found with his hands and feet chained to the bedposts. One girl was sucking his cock, the other was flicking red goldfish out of a jar and on to his stomach. The vibrant flapping of these fish excited him, for he realized that they were dying.

I was amused at the idea of a prostitute having to buy a bowl of tropical fish in order to appease a client's unreliable erection. But it was a warning; the police already had suspicions about the savagery which accompanied my sexual emotions. Even girls hired specifically to be whipped had complained. And so I determined to act more defiantly in order to scotch the lesser rumours circulated in my name. If the nature of my sexual gratifications was fabled as psycho-pathic, then I could at least hide behind the nature of an improbable fiction.

At that time I took to making excursions into the countryside. I was both in search of myself and others. At Avignon, Paris, Marseilles, I was distracted and later bored. My polysexual partners had experienced everything. There were men intimately versed in bondage, women who angled black cigarettes from scarlet lips, transsexuals who tinted their pubic hair blue or mauve. Money could procure any extravagance. It still does.

What I found in periods of travelling was a series of clues to my identity, and the way in which I connected with the world. I wasn't looking for anything or anyone; I let chance fall where it might. My stabs were at the random incidents in a plot we call reality. Sometimes I'd ride out for days, backtracking to my old retreats, Auvergne and Vichy, pushing my horse across the vast lavender fields of Provence, my face deadened by the wind, my mind streaming with an autonomous drift of consciousness. When I pulled up abruptly it was to confront myself. I was curious as to how thought evolved quite independent of my directing it. I'd be taking in the landscape, or thinking I was doing that, when all the time I was about to be surprised by some disarming implosion. And maybe death's like that. Only it's the reverse: you can't get back from the image that's absorbed you. You move off in a direction contrary to the body.

I'd be cutting into the taut blue distance, attempting to arrive at the vanishing point, when I'd break into an involuntary rage. I'd lash out at someone standing by the road just for being there, an action incidental to my frustration. I wanted to dominate the universe in the shape of the human ass, that constant preoccupation of mine, that overruling obsession that has taken me in and out of prison and asylum cells; that in all its variant forms riots through my unconscious. Sometimes I would imagine I was riding through a deep cleavage between hills. I would whip my horse to stimulate the ecstasy I knew at the pitch of orgasm. My cock was elephantine. It could take on a field of bulls and overpower them with its potency.

I'd stop off at hotels, lathered and dripping from the fury of my rides. The light of the hills burnished my face. The valleys were re-created in the lines under my eyes. My skin smelt of vineyards, mustard, lavender. If there was a young girl at the hotel I'd goose her. I wanted nothing more than to bend her over my knees and apply a slipper to her cheeks. And to work her up this way until she thought my entering her in my own manner perfectly natural.

But I tired of searching within myself. The autumn attracted me by its smell of rot and dissolution. Overripe conical pears scored by wasps, the thud of freckled windfalls in windy orchards, great skeins of starlings stringing over in billowing flocks. It was only then with the flying leaves, the mud-infested roads, the thinning out of nature's opulence that I felt earthed enough to be part of the cycle. If I look back it is to picture myself standing off the road in a field striped by ultramarine shadows, deciding to return to Paris. For a brief moment I ceased to feel part of the disinherited. And maybe that feeling lasted an hour. There was mud caking my boots. My black coat was spotted. But I didn't care. I had seen the whole universe flawed. Juice sluicing from fat green apples, leaves trodden underfoot into a matt carpet, grapes pulped in a vat. Nature was squeezing itself empty to await the iron grip of the cold. And I knew that fissure was visible in everything. It's in our minds and in our bodies, it travels beneath the earth and is traced out under the sea. It's to be found in space and it characterizes all the planets. And on another level it's the crack in the ass of Jeanne Testard, the young girl I was about to encounter in Paris.

Two

My mother warned me about men. And of course he's married too. They always are, the ones who request bizarre services in order to act out their fetishes. Usually I'm aware of the division between myself and the client's fantasy. He's come here to engage in a dialogue with himself; I'm simply the detached embodiment of that overruling need.

And it's not only men who come here. It's women too. They either want to be concealed in order to enlarge their repertory of lovemaking, or else they too desire my body. I've had them both. The Marquis and Madame de Sade.

Who am I? It's an enigma that's not resolved by a name. Jeanne Testard. I could be anyone. When I pronounce those syllables, no one answers. There's just the oval lake of a mirror reflecting the still-life which is its complementary partner. I'm no one, anyone, someone. If I want to make a red splash at life I shake my hair out for the reflection. I'm my own company. The people who come and go probably couldn't even describe me: the colour of my eyes (blue with hazel tints), the pointed arch to my lips, the way my left profile visibly disagrees with the right. Would it take a painter to index my facial characteristics?

Sometimes I see myself as an absence. When I'm in a black stockinged somersault, my legs almost truncated from my body, my mind orbiting a star risen within me, I come clear. I see myself looking down from the ceiling. I'm the Jeanne whc existed before he visited me. And perhaps I can describe him better than he would ever have identified me. Small, below the average height, but making up for this by an imperiousness, an assumed hauteur that caused him to stand out from the crowd. He wore grey and deep orange. His hairline was receding; his blue eyes stood out as lapis lazuli tinctures. His hands fidgeted. They didn't really match. But what made me note the details of his identity was the sense of presence he projected. You can walk through or round most people and they don't even register. They're there, but not as realities; they exist as volume, an undifferentiated mass pushing through the streets. They are neutralized by one's thoughts, which are bigger and more imposing in terms of the inner space they occupy. But there was something about this man which fixed my eyes to his and kept them there. I felt them go all the way in. I could see that no one had done that to him before.

Instinct told me to avoid him; but in a contradictory impulse I saw in him a means to self-discovery. There's a breaking point for all of us. We advance to the limits of the self and decide whether to go on or back. I was impelled forward. He had retained the two eyes I had thought to extract from his mid-brain. I was fixed in there and couldn't escape unless he let go. And that was why I went back with him. Even if he hadn't touched me I would have felt violated. That was his way. He could project his intentions to the point whereby one would have felt struck even if his hands had been tied. He slapped me with the taut edge of his mind.

He wasn't just anyone. If he'd pointed his head left I would have looked in that direction. And his wife really loved him. Renée-Pélagie de Montreuil. In her confessions to me she admitted to being his procuress. Unable to satisfy his rapacious needs, she had resigned herself to finding young people of both sexes who would not only appease, but also cultivate his sexual propensities. There was little beauty in Renée's features. But there was a luminosity, a sense of being lit up by the singular conviction in which she believed – a devotion to love – that brought out the concealed highlights in her face to which she wouldn't normally admit. We all

24

possess this hidden face. Our external features are a pentimento. They're the cover for what goes on inside.

Not only was Renée still in love with her husband, she developed a relationship with me. When I talked to her, her hands would run up my silk stockings. And all the time she made out that nothing was happening, but her fingers were feeling for the money I kept in my stocking-top beneath the black suspender strap. It turned her on, the improbable equation in her life of money and sex. After it was over she would cry. Nothing on this level had ever happened before, so she would claim. Her family were part of the old aristocracy. They resented the man she had married; they wanted to see the back of him. His scandalous licentiousness, his flagrant association with whores, all of these outraged them. De Sade would have raised a whip to his own mother's bottom; but I came to realize that while it was his overriding obsession, it was also a form of experimentation, a way of finding out how far he could go. All the time he was using it as a means to something else. There was going to come a point in his life when he'd have to review his sexual risks. Even if he couldn't see it, I knew he was advancing towards this point. What I discovered in him was a division between his sense of inner and outer reality. He'd be talking to me, but all the time he was somewhere else. This happens with some men, but with him the split was pronounced. He was going somewhere I couldn't follow. And at such times I had the sense he was using me. I was here and he was there; and there was nothing bridgeable in between. He might have been standing on the moon. I was on the bed arching my legs high in the hope of earthing him.

And Renée. I suppose her mother paid to have him watched and Renée intercepted correspondence, followed her husband about town on the trail of aleatory clues. She was searching for the impossible: a reformed husband. What she found was what she couldn't discredit: the accusatory voice of those who had been on the receiving end of intolerable brutality.

Of course we're paid; but there are limits. What de Sade required was not a body but a manipulative robot. He demanded more of himself than he could ever fulfil, while at the same time he attempted to annihilate his victim. The body is too limited, unserviceable for his needs. He wanted to be both himself and the other. 'I have destroyed everything in my heart which might have interfered with my pleasures.' The line is his. And he was its embodiment.

I'm a fan maker. I hand-paint little designs on silk: vignettes that suggest an idealized view of scenic countryside. Two lovers stand on an eyebrow-shaped bridge above a blue ripple of water. A line of poplars admits a house with open shutters through the trees. Living in the city there's something serene about composing fictional states. Sometimes I splash orange and gold leaves on grey silk and evoke the mood that accompanies autumn. And I have my special clients, those who come with news of their travels and order something exotically tropical – a plant, a bird, extravagant foliage, a cove set into a coast. And there are those who wish to isolate a fetish: two red lips closing over an erect penis; a voyeuristic eye focused on a couple engaged in intimacies on a sofa. And so it goes on. I create and I take commissions. My income is small, too small to cope with the way a city breaks into one's privacy, one's right to live independent of money. I'm conscious that I live with one foot toeing the dust at the edge of a precipice. That's what led to my meeting up with a man with whom I would not usually have had contact. And also I was curious. Each time I went out to sell myself I made believe that I was only pretending. I would stop at a certain mark; but then I'd go ahead and cut the ribbon on the pretence that this would be the last time. But the money proved useful and then came to be indispensable to my needs. I began to add decorative touches to my apartment, and to buy fabrics, perfumes, silk lingerie. I could put on a bright red lipstick and catch eyes in the street. It was a great feeling under a blue March sky, to know that I was someone, not just anyone in the great anonymous crowd.

But he went too far. I was frightened from the first. He insisted on having his chauffeur take us to his place. I didn't recognize the streets we drove through. I realized that in my time in Paris I had come to know only the smallest area in a vast labyrinth of interconnected streets. The day outside seemed unreal. The people going about their ordinary routines seemed portentous. I couldn't be sure that they and I belonged to the same planet. Things came at me in flashes. A church, a florist's, someone crossing the road and losing a green hat in the process. And the bits didn't really stick. It was like they wouldn't go into my mind and stay there. I couldn't see the chauffeur's face. He wore dark glasses and a hat tilted a shadow over his profile. Neither of the two men spoke. We accelerated through arrondissements, the tension building, my wrong decision turning on me in a silent reproach.

He had a house set back off the street. I was to learn later that it was south of the river, beyond the Luxembourg Gardens. A wrought-iron gate was set into a high wall. There were spikes on the top to deter possible intruders. The house was concealed by its own silence. A blue shadow played over the white walls. It was juniper interrupting the flow of light.

I was led to a room on the first floor and left alone with him. He was using his cold silence to unnerve me. I had lost the authority I usually asserted over a client. I had become someone answerable to an unreasoning mania. He had got me fixed and knew it. He proceeded to lock the door and then open a panel inserted into the wall. He pointed to a second room inside the first: smaller, compact, washed by a red bulb.

Stepping inside there was like going someplace else. When he came in behind me, I realized for the first time that I was trapped. I was standing in a room within a room. Like a Chinese puzzle, each subsequent space was reduced in size. The act of recession excited him. It was as though he had already entered me by the extension of a psychic probe. I was losing body temperature; if I'd looked at my toes I would have expected to find blue ice cubes. The last room was hung with black drapes. On the wall were instruments of discipline. There was an armoury of whips, birch rods, and thongs whose metal tips were to be heated in the fire before use. The walls were covered with pictures depicting perverse sexual positions: a woman up on her haunches was being whipped at the same time as she sucked the cock of a man kneeling before her. I saw these things as though they had found me rather than I them. My mind was responsive to his mesmeric control. I could only have come this far by unconsciously obeying his dictates.

27

I wasn't prepared for what happened. I mean the body occupies a space; it functions in accordance with rights of privacy. We usually cross those barriers when we sustain an injury, and then we realize we've fallen out of orbit; we've exceeded our limitations.

We didn't know each other and yet he was going to have me savagely whip him before he performed the same on me. It was like taking part in a film which held no meaning for one of the participants. The silence was taut; when it snapped it was the sound of a whip lashing his back. A red stripe and a blue, a red stripe turning blue, and so on. . . . I aimed the lash and it came back at me without tension. I could feel nothing. I was too light-handed for him; his imprecations demanded I savage him so he could administer a reciprocal ferocity. He was like a man praying to himself, a spider eating its own legs and celebrating the consequent mutilation. And for the first time I realized I could strike someone. There was a momentum building up in me with which I connected. I was suddenly conscious of how one can overshoot. From being uninvolved, disinclined to participate, separated from the experience by what I took to be an instinctive loathing, I became someone channelling their aggression into a narrow strip of welted flesh. I wanted to make him disappear; I thought if I kept on striking him the reality of the situation would shatter like a glass. I'd find myself back in my work-room amongst my brushes, my fabrics, with the light streaming in as a continuous visitor. I wanted to burst into tears, but the conflicting emotion of anger was stronger. This man was nothing to me. I told myself I could break his back and run. I'd never be the same person again, but I could do it. I knew I'd go out to a street I wouldn't recognize, I'd look up at a sky that didn't belong, I'd go so far into an unknown quarter and then break down.

But instead, I just went on hitting him with monotonous regularity. There was blood streaming down his back. He was jerking off in tune with the pain. It couldn't be me who was doing this. I was dreaming myself. I was somewhere else, painting a red butterfly on blue silk.

Suddenly the crack of the whip was occurring without my

directing it. I didn't have the strength to continue, but the reverberations were exploding inside my ears. I was being slapped outside and inside my head. I could almost hear the click of his thoughts. He was going to transpose his madness so that I suffered. Lift off on his up-beat kick, and turn on me with it. He needed the high of being humiliated in order to abuse me. An interval would represent a lowering of tension.

And I followed. I took up his place and gagged in expectation of the pain. He slashed the back of my dress open. I doubled over a chair, not believing this, refusing to associate my real self with this humiliation. It couldn't be me and so I didn't realize the pain. He was hitting someone or something else, a sack, a chair, a body. It was all the same. Objects smash like we do. In my mind I was walking down a sunlit street, window-shopping. I was in a black dress with a black bow in my hair. I stopped to look at window displays: an orange blouse on a model; a jeweller's card of earrings; bottles of wine. One – a café with people outside at tables, two – a grocer's, three – a funeral parlour's opaque glass. I was making rapid transitions. The pain was incidental. I had cut myself off so completely I couldn't feel. I remember wondering at his useless waste of energy, the way he scratched up on a blackboard in red chalk the number of lashes he had administered. He used a knife-point on himself, the lacerations forming involved contours of superficial wounds.

He was enraged by my failure to show either pleasure or pain. I was an object he could never forgive; if I'd become a subject he would have killed me. When he stopped I couldn't get up. I wasn't going to have him see me broken. I was like a bird without wings, a swan that can't rise from the lake to migrate with the serpentine festoon blackening the autumn sky. I was to be the straggler left to die on the slopes of a mountain summit.

I was dulled and insensible to what was happening. The silence closed over me like a wave. I was being lifted by heavy surf as it ran for the beach. I could hear my body grate to a halt on the sharp shingle. I was left there like the dead mule I had seen rolled across the beach in childhood. Its bulk had been dragged over reefs; the sea had acted on it as a surgeon might.

I wasn't prepared for what came next. He was telling me he wanted me from behind, and that I was still a virgin in terms of the sex he would inflict on me. I could feel his urgency pressing against me; the delirium in his blood hummed. He was going to force himself into me, impale me with his lust. I lacked the strength to protest. I was shocked into submission. Whatever happened it wouldn't be me who was the recipient of his desire. If he entered me it would be another person, someone pretending to be me. I wasn't even tense, I was just indifferent. What would once have revolted me, seemed now to be something of inconsequence. But I did feel the pain. The disproportion must have been huge: his width against my constriction, his need against my contraction. I was being opened up and it burnt. His breathing was fast and irregular. I had the feeling he would have gone through me if he could – bored a hole from one side to the other. He wanted to kill sex in the act of having it, because it failed to realize a future. It immersed him in the present. 'What we are doing here is only the image of what we would like to do', he wrote to me later. But forceful buggery wasn't to be repealed by his philosophic notions. They came later with an aftertaste as bitter as lemon. They continued like his life.

I was impaled. He had entered me as no one had done before. There was not the least condescension to my pain. My anaesthetic of shock and detachment was wearing off. He was boring into me. I kept on thinking he must be near to his crisis, but each time he delayed, backed out of his climax and resumed his rhythm. He was watching me and watching himself. He wanted me to be him and for him to be me. It was his isolation that disturbed his sense of pleasure. He needed to be both and he was only one. 'The pleasure of the senses is always regulated in accordance with the imagination.' He wrote me that from prison.

I couldn't take any more. I was being crippled. I decided to contract on him and make him come like that. I squeezed my muscles and constrained him. He was trapped. He couldn't get up or out. The pressure I asserted made him gasp. He discharged a string of obscenities and ejaculated. He was mad at the end. He had lost the idea of the future and was defused by his inability to regain his excitement.

My only thought was to get out. I wanted to walk so fast and for so long that I would lose myself for ever, end up in another country. And who do two people become after an act of enforced intimacy? There isn't anywhere to go. I'd have liked to have dematerialized, left him there facing his emptied vacuum. Instead we were over-present. He was sweating profusely. Droplets were sparkling on his torso. And there was nothing but hatred between us. Or if it wasn't outright animosity it was paranoid estrangement. We were left as two objects, statues beached by the tide and rubbed over shingle. I could feel the blood streaming down the backs of my legs. Could I forgive a man this humiliation? And could he forgive my having been a partner to it? We were stranded without speech. I could taste death inside my mouth.

I suppose we both recognized that his only recourse was to kill me. But in his perverse way he needed a witness to his mania in order to authenticate his depravity. He had only his eyes, his hands, his motives. I multiplied them. Together we represented four eyes, four hands, four legs, two backs, two bottoms. And each time the story was imparted to someone else, so the components would multiply. His contradictory nature wanted to be both private and universal. He wanted to live outside the law and at the same time have it know of his sexual propensities.

I doubt he was ever a good lover. He expected of sex the impossible: the annihilation of his fantasy in the act of possessing it. Instead it eluded him. He could never achieve physical gratification because he faced a mirror rather than the body of his partner. Each time he threw himself against the glass, ending up more fascinated by his wounds than by those which he had inflicted on others, he was left with the idea of pain as representing pleasure. I suppose it was this which led him to be indifferent to the suffering he had created in his victims. By living out their roles he assumed that he had suffered for them. How could they bring charges against him, lock him up in a madhouse cell, when his only injury was to abuse himself? This may have been the reason that he was unable to stop himself. I was just one in a chain of random selections.

And there were other facets of sex that gave him kicks. The

deconsecration of the host by satanic liturgy. I fought against that. He wanted to pass a black wafer to me tongue to tongue.

I don't know how I found myself outside again. It was only then that the pain alerted me to what had happened. And when it did, it bit into my nerves. It felt like I had re-entered reality after a period away. I could hardly stand. I collapsed on to a bench. A wad of notes had been tucked into my leather boot. There wasn't any relationship between my pain and this payment. I didn't hate the man. I hated myself. If I needed to confess what had happened, it was because I couldn't contain it. The last hours had established a new terrifying geometry within me. My inner space had fragmented and I sat amongst its debris. I'd have to rebuild the structure and I was conscious I would never get it right again. The foundations had moved; the walls were fissured.

I must have blacked out. When I came to I could hear a voice asking me what had happened. The tone was objective, but at the same time solicitous. It was then that I found myself at a police station. I was talking to myself, deliriously but articulately. They assumed I was addressing them; a man kept note of what I was saying. I wondered why they wanted to record my speech. Everything I had undergone came out. His name, his height, the colour of his eyes, the manner of his voice, the black-draped room, the whips, thongs. It came out like a speeded-up film monologue. Words were tripping over words, but I wasn't hysterical. The whole thing poured from me like an exorcism. I was telling in order to be light again. In order to rebuild on the site of ruins.

The man across the desk seemed pleased with what I was relaying. I felt like saying he had no right to be taking such a close interest in my story. I just wanted to deliver it and go. But he was curious. He opposed the stream of my narrative. He kept on forcing me to backtrack. He wanted to know what sort of sex I had experienced, and was I absolutely sure I had been sodomized. I went into it with excruciating detail. If they showed signs of disbelieving me, I raised my voice. I wasn't going to be contradicted: I knew what had happened. I lifted up my skirt for them to see the red and blue horizontals which had eaten into my body. That induced a silence which made me frightened. They must have lost interest in my story. Their eyes were fixed on me. They wanted to escort me to a cubicle but I refused. I didn't want to undergo yet another form of isolation; my purpose was in delivering the action of events.

I knew as I spoke to them that something irreparable had happened to me. They were quiet because they didn't wish to alarm me. And I carried on. I was like a rattlesnake; my crepitaculum vibrated with anger. I would have liked my words to have notched up bullet-holes. I was telling them something they would never hear again. There would be other cases, variations; but mine would never come again. My story would last as long as my breath.

I was taken home. I sat in the back of the car silent, as I had been when his chauffeur drove us across town. I had said nothing then, and I maintained that reserve now. The streets were dark and empty. People could be seen leaving a theatre, a cinema. Red and blue neons flickered on and off across the road. It had begun to rain. Big, sparkling flashes were caught in the headlights. They hung there like lozenges suspended against the black. The streets were glazed, unreal until we came to the one in which I lived. I couldn't understand how they had found it. What had brought the driver here? I wanted to tell them to turn round and make for a different arrondissement, a quarter of impenetrable alleys; but they were quite sure about their sense of location. One of them got out and opened a door for me. He didn't seem to notice that it was raining. Droplets sat on his shoulders like tadpoles, and made little flurries into figures of eight. I recognized the street as my own. There was the warehouse opposite; the pink shaled stucco of a house-front; lion-faced mascarons; the high-rise flats with the stairwell lit all night; and looking up, the room above my own screened by a dark green curtain. Who was it lived there? They never showed. I would have to live out their narrative. Take nocturnal walks, sit up all night thinking into the rectangular window surface, see the day arrive red on blue above the city. It was me. I stood there in the street a long time after the car had driven away. It must have been me. I knew the way up the stairs to the second floor. The light stayed on awhile and then snapped dead.

Three

I've decided the easiest way is silence. If I'm not heard then I can concentrate on my inner voice. I can wall myself up and trap that resonance as a fly vibrates in a spider's web. I'm insulated by stone. I'm a living ammonite at its centre. If I was to stop thinking, the sound of my heartbeat would be like that of a hammer knocking on the other side of the wall. I'd never sleep again. As it is I dream. Tropical jungles spring up in my cell. A strangulating liana turns into a trunk-thick green snake. In the suspended, slow-action takes of nightmare, I watch the wedged arrowhead close on me. When contact is made the forked tongue impales me to a tree. The poison injected into me makes my body swell. My legs turn to bloated cacti; my torso grows inflated. I become like a rubber balloon pushing against the obduracy of stone.

And so I write. Not as most people do, openly displaying their materials on a surface: a word-processor, pen and paper; but as someone for whom writing is as much a criminal act as the sexual offences which brought him here.

I write on a scroll of bandage in microscopic handwriting. The length of bandage measures thirty-nine metres. At night I roll it into a tight spiral and deposit it behind a stone in the wall. A novel that reeks of dust, mortar, the mildew that comes of confinement. Its constriction conceals its danger. Contained within that cylindrical, elongated finger is the detonative flash that will revolutionize sexuality. Keeping it private allows me to live with its momentum. It will take the creation of a new species to accommodate my vision of a sexual vocabulary. I can envisage sex through every organ. And why not through the aperture of the eye? The male psychology is visually oriented. Seeing generates excitement. Suppose we could have sex with our eyes, our sense of balance, our neurons, electrons, protons, enzymes, DNA, and our external faculties; the navel, crook of the shoulder, the friction of skin back to back, ass to ass. Anywhere. Beneath the fingernails, toenails. Within the area of hearing, the projection of feeling. There are so many unexplored zones of sexual union: psychic and physical.

When I came to the Bastille I was someone else. I had never experienced opposition to my needs. My voice dictated; my impulses were obeyed. But once inside I was stripped of every command. I became vulnerable like a child. I was deprived of human rights. I was treated like someone who had no connection with a past. My power, income, sexual motivation, aesthetic refinement, hatred of the cold, fear of constrictive spaces, fastidious washing habits were expected to be erased immediately on admission.

I feared insanity. The dark of the cell would become a wall of rats that ran over me like surf. The air was thick. I couldn't breathe. It seemed to have the consistency of horsehair. And my mind span crazily like a record played at the wrong speed. I was in danger of losing identity. I was no longer me.

I raved. Hallucinating I saw the large rooms at La Coste. I believed if I closed my eyes for long enough and then opened them again, I would be somewhere else. I watched my life projected on the wall like cut-ups from a film. I wanted to follow the sequential flashes back to the source from which they originated. Why do we live things to which we can't return? This separation in itself is cause for insanity. I am here and what I've known is over there.

When I was forced into exile, when I was living in Savoy after the scandal in Marseilles, I used to try and locate the crime I was carrying. Where was it? In what part of my mind or body did it hide? I was being hunted for something which was neither visible nor tangible. Once a crime is committed it becomes a component of the imagination. The police were going to arrest me for an act which had no visible identity. They were going to accuse me of concealing evidence. It was as though the act was within me in the way a dealer might swallow cocaine inside a knotted condom in order to evade the customs. I was marked with an invisible cross. And of course they came. They surrounded the house at Chambéry, and I was conveyed to the redoubtable hilltop fortress of Miloans. It was impossible to justify the circle of soldiers and armed police which hemmed me in. They could have been attempting to put down a riot: instead they were waiting for me. They were men who knew nothing of my sensibility, nothing of my past nor my intended future. They stuck to me like flies. They wanted to see me humiliated in order to vindicate their own limitations, their own inadequacies.

My vulnerability enhanced their false sense of solidarity. From my cell I could see the distant Alps. Their peaks were patchy with pink snow in the clear red sunset that blazed across the landscape. They were uninhabitable needles, remnants of primal catastrophe – the blasting of planetary megatons across the universe. There was no consolation inside or out. I wrote letters. I appealed, I importuned help against the impending crisis. And as I wrote so the danger I was in became a reality. Words magnified my condition. In a way I had chanced upon the evocation that language implies. Words had come to me when my hands were empty. They were quite suddenly there; they vibrated at my touch. I had now to choose what to do with them. They were already the unconscious clue to my future. Without them, my mind disintegrated into chaos.

I had little doubt that I was to be consigned to oblivion. I was told that the nature of my crime allowed for no appeal. And if I was to be returned to the French authorities I might end up being treated like a circus bear, a patchy, ursine rag prodded with sticks. Rage was my one lead back to reality and I directed it at everyone who came near me: the Sardinian authorities, the prison governor, my stringy undernourished servant. I tipped my pen with it. My words carried bee stings;

36

they were barbed, venomous, charged with an irate explosive calculated to blow up in the recipient's eyes. What else could I do but lash out at the paralysing experience of having others decide on my future? It was like being the blind passenger in a car driven head-on at a wall.

What I ask is what no one is prepared to understand. Let me read you an extract from a letter. I don't know who 'you' are. Any reader is a chance affair. The time in which you live is peculiarly your own. All we share is the agonizing realization of how separate we are. As you read this your own life is disappearing. Mine had slowed to a blank cliff-face on which I tore my nails.

You who decide whether something is a crime or not, you who have people executed in Paris for actions that would be honoured in the Congo, tell me why I find sea-shells on mountain-tops and ruins on the sea-bed. You who instate laws demanding conformity, fail to realize that the world needs good and evil. How can I put it? It's the difference between light and dark, and the balance. We need both. You refuse to understand differentiation. You call what differs from you crime; but isn't it unjust to punish actions which are justified by a different sensibility? Would you jeer at a blind man, ridicule gays, throw a petrol bomb through the window of a man dying of AIDS, persecute the poor, mock the deformed, push a cripple into the traffic? And the answer is YES. In attempting to vindicate your prejudicial fears and inadequacies you penalize those who have the courage to live out what you have repressed.

What I detest is the cold. I can't think or write in the gelid temperature to which I'm subjected. If I lay my hands on the pipes intended for my warmth, then I realize how I've grown into a subtext for the machinations of others. I'm deprived of the right to think or speak for myself. Other people lie for me. They invent my voice and my feelings. I begin to assume I have a robotic double. There's an Inspector Marais involved in all this, a man attracted to me by a fixed, psychopathic hatred. It's possible to free oneself of many things, but an unreasoning, inflexible motivation to harm another is the most dangerous of all impulses. It accounts for the one victim in the crowd at rush-hour. There is no protest, only the split-second realization it had to happen.

I have in my wife's mother and in this man who is paid to implement her wishes, a force of enquiry which hunts me from place to place. I'm there in the dark and they find me like a laser. They have the armed police arrive at night, headlights blazing; a bunch of thugs spilling out of a car.

I'm told my wife has tried to reach me here. She came dressed as a man, but couldn't fool the guards. Renée has this sense of recklessness. Certain she'll never find another husband, afraid of the suffocation which living with her mother entails, hungry for the eroticism I taught her, her freedom depends on mine. She defied her mother to do this and, on being exposed, wrote angry letters to the governor. An abuse which owed something to me in its refusal to consider any alternative to its driving monomania.

I have to fight against apathy. Writing and anger are healthy antidotes to breakdown. And when you're first confined to a cell, you think there's no way out. The walls are too close; at night they move in for the kill, and by day they are indifferent. Then one day you see clean through them; the stone is suddenly transparent. A door asserts itself and beyond that is a landscape detached from the surrounding countryside. You've been there before, but never expected to encounter it again. There's a mass of cherry blossom like an unruly pink dune screening a house in which a· woman in black silk lingerie is making up before a mirror. She'll do anything you want if you can only get there. She's expecting you, but your time isn't hers. She is anticipating you now, running a red fingernail over her black panties, exciting herself in preparation for your arrival. The house is so close you could be there in five minutes. The door is open, admitting a late red sunlight. She has prepared everything: the chain, the satin gloves, the whip. She is frantic for you to appease her urgency. She makes a long-legged somersault. You know you can get there. It's just a matter of shifting barriers, translating one dimension into another.

And quite suddenly I was free. The door between the room in which I dined and the kitchen to which I was denied access, was open. It had been arranged by someone on the inside. Below the window was a short drop to the sloping terrain, and the blue night air rushed at my face as I tumbled out into another element. There were men standing off in the dark. They came out of the shadows. They might have been answering a sexual need, coming together under the trees in the night. Only they were men brought into my service; hired killers who would protect me on the journey back to France. The night air was cold; I was shocked into the reality of what was happening by my glacial intake of breath. We travelled on horseback until meeting up with a car on the border road. No one spoke. On the lower slopes an owl opened up in a thicket. The distance between Miloans and the frontier was a short one and we had made Lyons by daybreak. A red sky hung above the sleeping town. I was free but only in terms of how I could use that concept mentally.

And so it begins all over again. I can't remedy my needs; they are stronger than I and demand attention. They travel with me and I with them; our traffic is consummated through acts of reckless subversion.

And my wife? Let me return to her. And there are children. A son who will inherit my genes, my disposition? It wasn't Renée that I intended to marry, it was her sister Anne. And I enjoyed both of them, provoking by my actions the prickly outrage of their mother, the undying anger of a baying wolf. I wanted to travel with Anne and arouse Renée to a sexual jealousy which would have her eager to accept even the most unpalatable of my sexual tastes. And she did. She waited for me with a panther's hunger. I would blindfold her, tie her legs together over her head and have my various ways with her. And sometimes I would introduce a third person, someone who would make love to me simultaneous with my making love to Renée. Knowing my aberrations excited her. It was a flagrant refutation of her mother's social aspirations, to be pinned on the bed by someone with an underworld reputation. And the knowledge of my pathological search for partners did nothing to dispirit her. Renée was a willing accomplice to those actions of mine which brought me into conflict with the law. She would go out on the streets dressed as a man and operate as a pimp. This was our habit in Paris. Dressed in gold earrings, a green suit, a wide tie and white shirt, she would proposition for me.

And when alone, I get to thinking about what motivated her to adopt a way of expression so alien to her person. Love makes a stranger of us all. Did she act in this manner to please me, or did I provide the role in order to realize something latent within her? The ambiguities are inexhaustible. Renée feared the oppressive authority of her parents. She would have followed a lion by its tail to be free of her past. I was not seeking to escape from the body politic; I was intending to delete its principles. My voice is an anarchic one demanding change. I will write in blood on my shirt: 'Only he who looks to the future, looks cheerfully.'

From Lyons I travelled on to La Coste, the road eaten up by the Mercedes, the windy French poplars pointing to blue sky breaks. How long could it last? I knew I would be hunted, that word of my escape would soon be out. But I refused to act like a fugitive. I was someone; I would not have that subtracted for me. Cows were being let out into a field; they bolted into the meadow which was a child's painting of yellow buttercups, white clover, an invasive forest of needling thistles. Further on a solitary goat stood by the roadside under the increasingly blue sky.

Being driven across the countryside is a useful aid to perception. What flashes up at one is a world parallel to the constant vignettes that evolve by way of inner dialogue. Watching out of a car window is like being in two places at once, and both are verifiable. At one point I had the driver stop. I couldn't control my impulse to run full tilt at a meadow. I lay in the tall grass, my hands rooting at the earth, the sharp scent of wild garlic cutting at my perception. It was one of those moments. The little things that go to make up a life.

My theatre at La Coste still lacked completion but was advanced enough for me to stage the first of my many attempts to write a successful play. Renée was prepared to use her income to accommodate the architectural flights of my imagination. I wanted to live according to my dictum: 'Every man is a tyrant when he fucks.'

I waited only for the autumn to arrive. I wanted to establish within the walls at La Coste the insulated environment I had known as a child at Saumane, when my uncle the abbé closed the gates of the château on winter and the world, and was free to engage without distraction in the sexual pleasures he had devised for the entertainment of himself and his friends. It was there I saw a young man with his erect cock speckled with caviar, and girls engaged in multiple sex with two or three men. And there was nothing to disturb the household. We lived like people detached from the world. We dreaded the returning spring, the efflorescent renewal of pink almond and cherry blossom, the revitalization of a dormant community, the extinction of the great fires and our journey back to the light.

And I wanted to reinstate the idea of a self-contained universe at La Coste. We had the money to detach ourselves and pay for silence. I had begun by experimenting with an adolescent troupe in the theatre. Young girls dressed in black basques and black suspenders acted out one of my plays in which a young boy was positioned in a crocodile's jaws and beaten. The effect was brutally surreal. The narrative of the play involves a journey to the islands. Two men in white linen suits, both of them subscribing to a cocaine habit, sit in the stern of a boat negotiating a creek. They keep their eyes trained for the jetty they know is stationed beneath a massive swathe of foliage. It's hot and the crew are stripped naked. At a point in the narrative when. . . .

I wanted to live out the reality of disappearing from the world. La Coste was intended to become a centre for the development of a new species. Children would be born in time who would inherit no other values than those propagated within the structure of my teachings. If I could, I would have had the house situated at the most inaccessible point on the earth. Now that aircraft and cars have dissected all impenetrable routes, opened up all improbable spaces, location has to be buried in inner rather than outer space. It's in those quarries that we sink codified systems, bury our psychosexual secrets, live out our true impulses.

Everything was made ready at the château for a winter of uninterrupted pleasure. By keeping a low profile, repressing my natural inclination towards ostentation, and observing an absolute quiet about the place for the declining summer months, I was able to prepare my scheme for the coming winter. The local residents weren't properly aware that I had returned. I kept myself indoors, writing, overseeing the construction of the theatre. Workmen in and about the premises were constant; they were a feature of a house which needed continuous attention.

My wife was here sometimes but absent for longer intervals. It was a time of big storms. The blue of high noon would give way to a tin-sharp light that would turn a brownish-purple. Thunder shook us in the early afternoons, reverberating without warning across the landscape. It sounded like the sky was a window breaking from the centre outwards. Hot rain steamed across the courtyard, a clammy sauna which vaporized in hissing clouds. It wasn't like any other summer I had experienced; even the distant sound of a car on the road caused one to start, fearing the return of thunder.

I was growing older; I half recognized this in my face and then forgot about it later. My sex was volcanic; it came from a laval interior. My need overrode any attempted moderation of that impulse. There was a small flower garden at La Coste; the musty late-summer scent of roses, stock, rosemary, thyme, lavender flooded into a heady suffusion after the abrupt rains. I liked to breathe in that saturation; the earth was aspiring to fullness before a yellow and red note was sewn into the vineyards. And I drank, not inordinately, but with a curiosity to taste the sunlight which had lived in the wine for ten years before uncorking. That summer in which I had seen the grapes growing fat was a time of imprisonment. And now I tasted my confinement again in the black, tangy bouquet. I had learnt to live in myself inside a cell like fetid water in a tank. I didn't want anyone near me; my humiliation was complete. I had discovered that to write was to invent a world which wouldn't have existed otherwise. And was it any the less real for being imagined? Aren't there multiple textures of consciousness? Behind the one film, there's another being shown to a different viewer, and so on. It was the injustice of restraint I tasted in the black sun of that summer. At that time I wrote pamphlets in opposition to every piece of legislation that threatened man's individual liberty. I went at it like a knife slashing a silk dress. I spoke of the need for man to educate himself in the psychology of others and not to maintain hypocritically a stance of immunization from crime. Which of us does not hide his aberrations with a secrecy he hopes is impenetrable? I denounced governments, oligarchies, plutocracies. It was like throwing snow in midsummer. My gestures evaporated. I was an animal skinning itself on the bars of a cage.

The rain was building again overhead. A huge magenta corolla had worked its way into view. This time I didn't intend to beat a quick retreat indoors. I wanted to be washed clean of the summer months and prepare myself for the coming autumn. There was an absolute concentration in what I intended to do. In my mind I was already assembling the selected local inhabitants in the main hall. Renée and my pimp, Nanon, would have chosen them for those peculiarities which appeal to me. Women and young men selected for their femininity and for their ignorance of the ways of sex I would initiate them into would form the nucleus of my stable. I needed also the ugly to serve as an opposing tension, and two older women renowned for their sexual expertise, who could participate in the sort of riotous three in a bed which I needed as a periodic catharsis. I was already preoccupied with their figures, responses to my demands, inhibitions, awakening fetishes. And if they stayed they would be taken care of. I am a man who can only reach compassion through sexual cruelty. Once I have arrived at that place I realize the true nature of my identity. And sometimes I have to go too far to find a corrective to my behaviour.

I looked up; the warm rain was smacking red petals off the roses. The rhythm was slow, metronomic, a prelude to the delayed deluge, the torrential lash which would arrive like the sparkle in a sheeting wall of surf. And then it smoked in, beating my head and shoulders, washing the landscape out with its unremitting force. I shelled my clothes and stood there naked, half doubled by an intoxicating volubility. I wanted to feel rain as the earth receives it. I was hurrying towards autumn in rapid cancellations of the days. The vine's fruition would be mine and my blood would be decanted into sex. I would hear wolves come down from the heights. And if I walked out one day and found a car waiting at the back of the property, or a blind horse staring on the road, I'd know that it was time.

I went back in, exhilarated by the downpour's friction on my skin. I was excited. My thoughts must have swum like bright, tropical fish in clear water. I caught Renée in a state of half undress. I scooped her generous breasts out of a transparent bra, and carried her from her dressing-table chair to the bed. She squealed and kicked her stockinged legs in the air. She flipped over on to her stomach, her black panties providing a translucent film between me and her bottom. I started to spank her with my hand, imparting a nettled rash to her cheeks, and you know the rest. These sessions sent me into hiding in my own house. I faced storms in my mirror. I kept alone that night. I knew that the coming autumn was going to take me deeper into the labyrinth than I had ever journeyed before. I could smell singed leather, fur, the acrid reek of dope; my senses were already anticipating the scents of sex, fear, sweat, of drugs smoked to heighten or nullify the nerves. I was demented that night. I shut myself up and sat outstaring the mirror as I might have a big cat. One of us would have to break. And the dawn found me still there, burning with unresolved tension.

When they were brought here that autumn, the countryside turning the colour of a fox pelt hung up to dry, the entire region involved in the grape harvest, I was aware of the cyclic nature of my life. I would go on doing this because there was no other way. I have walked down so many corridors and opened the doors to right and left and found the rooms empty. I'm not wanted there. There's a chair, a table, the few incidentals left by a vanished person. I watch myself walking towards a future in which very few can share.

The supplies started coming in before the weather turned.

Not ostentatiously, but with a regularity that allowed the cellars and freezers to be stocked for a four-month period. This time I intended our isolation to be total. I didn't want any leak to get through to the neighbouring villages. Not a word. Lorries backed up into the courtyard and were unloaded. I wanted to lack for nothing. If I was an oddity, an aberrant individual hunted for the form of sex to which he subscribed, then I was set upon indulging my idiosyncrasies within a framework of my own making.

Listening in the quiet of the house at night, I could make believe that I was at the world's end. I would go into the theatre and sit down on stage, having arranged for a single red spotlight to find me in the dark. I was happy at such times. Inflatable Japanese dolls sat behind me as a backdrop. And here I could act out the psychodrama which raged within me. 'I am the only one of my species.' The echo-chamber built into the sound-system made provision for the liturgical voice effects which I required. 'I am the only one of my species.' The distortion came back to me. Here I could isolate myself in the context of a man living against the grain of history. Once you have seen through anything which is false it turns upon you with enmity. The status quo is a drugged zoo-captive lion. Its limp testicles sag. What it manifests is the impotence that comes of having the carotid artery severed.

Sometimes I'd stay in the theatre for the entire night. I'd write or act out the parts I'd devised for others. It was always like that in prison or out. I was about to be acclaimed as the leader of a new race. I really believed that. It was in the air. The autumn and winter would consolidate my claim. And at the same time my need to be solitary increased; I slept alone and eschewed Renée's advances. Something in me was acquiring energy. I was untouchable. A revolution was finding completion in my blood. My dreams were full of the recurring image of a man being led out through an underground corridor to face the light of a packed stadium. He knew he must prepare himself to address the assembled crowd. He was the hero that my detractors had tried so hard to eliminate.

For the first week I wouldn't look at the additions to the household. I knew that six girls and four young men had agreed to spend the winter at La Coste. I imagined them. It was easier that way. And if I really tried hard enough they would materialize as the exact counterparts of my imagining. And they would never forget me. Could you?

On the first night I agreed to meet them, I kept my back turned on the company. I addressed the opposite wall. I wanted to make it clear that there was no appeal. In consenting to come here they had made themselves mine. I wanted to inculcate in them a belief in depersonalization. I was not to be thought of as a person, but a need. My name was never to be spoken in their presence. If in time they turned against me they would have to prosecute an absence. The château would be empty by the returning spring. I might be anywhere, leaving my minimal staff to maintain the property.

Renée and Nanon have chosen well. There are three blondes, a redhead and a brunette amongst the girls. The boys are androgynous. They are interchangeable with the girls. I will have them wear lipstick and the lightest Shiseido make-up. A little black under the eyes, a dusting of porcelain on the cheeks. At times I contemplate creating the first child to be conceived by a man. It would prove the ideal successor to my title. Beyond that, there's no greater perversion.

And now the rains have set in. I occupy my time with writing plays and recapitulating my past. How is it that the present alters the things we have done? It's never the same event when words recall it for me. It's as though we live two lives. The second evaluates what the first intended, but neither establishes a belief in reality.

In the mornings I visit my seraglio. Such gestures at least suggest that I am human. And as the weeks progress there is almost a rivalry in their willingness to be selected for certain roles. Only through brutally inflicting pain can the compassion in me be realized. I have to break someone down to be able to feel for them. And to indulge in my propensities requires money and influence, both of which are available to me. My sequestrated existence appears to hang on Renée's ability to extort money from her parents. If they cannot lock me up, then they are happiest when I am living in isolation from the world. They know nothing of my universal assets.

46

Last night I overreached in my dark-room. I didn't know I'd gone too far until afterwards. I was sweating like someone who's been running all night in a dream, pursuing a street to a dead-end. I saw what I'd done from a remove. It was like watching someone else on film. I'd used the birch too liberally; her body was slatted with deep cuts. It looked like a red and mauve Venetian blind had been impressed on her skin. When she was untied, she tried to escape, but there's never any way out from the bondage cell over which I officiate. And there was blood running down my back. I'd had myself whipped to orgasm. And now this girl and others complain of pregnancy, as if my way of having sex could do that.

Sometimes I wish I'd had a tiger, a leopard, a panther introduced into the house. Its presence would have served as a corrective to escape. As it is I entertain my guests with a theatre constructed for the mad. Here they can witness live sex acts, histrionic diatribes against institutions, two figures crawling around in sacks looking to find the way to the centre of the world.

47

Four

I couldn't believe it. I used to ask myself over and over again
what it was in me that was attracted to him. Those of us who
went to La Coste were propositioned. We weren't recruited,
thrown into a lorry and driven off to a barracks. We went
because there was something within us that wanted to find
expression. It's taken time for me to realize that. We came not
only from the surrounding villages, but from as far as Paris
and Marseilles. Word had spread about his activities. And it
wasn't that he paid well or in excess of others for the services
he required, it was more that he had come to represent a cult.
We were fascinated by what we heard said of his obsessive
fetishes, his deserted country home, the shaded plexiglass
windows of a car which was rumoured to be driven by a
transvestite.

We heard that he had resigned himself to a life of isolation
broken only by intermittent forays across the border. He was
like a storm that kept to the edges and wouldn't centre itself
above the plain. None of us in the gay bars had ever seen him,
but we had heard of him. He was spoken of as a man of great
refinement – but odd. His moods could switch perceptibly.
Someone said his split was like watching a solution change
colour; a moody violet might turn to a clear, blindingly
concentrated fluid. And then his mania would be directed
towards sex. Or was it that? We were told all sorts of things.

That he was a coprophiliac, a misogynist, that he was impotent, necrophiliac, that he cross-dressed and fucked cows in their winter stalls. We didn't know. No one knew.

But just by waiting, we knew that in time he would show up. The car would be left parked outside the bar; all eyes would centre on it. And the man's reserve, his apparent indifference to the company, the bottle of Dom Perignon cradled in an ice-bucket to his right, his eyes constantly returning to a book open on the table, all of these apparent diversions contributed to his implacable aura. He was so stand-offish, so unapproachable, that we, if we dared, jumped into his web like suicidal flies. And he always affected surprise. 'If you're that crazy, then you deserve what you get.' I'm sure that's what he said, or maybe I've got the wrong person. There were so many. But it must have come from him. Everything about him was memorable. He used to say in his moments of compassion that one should be sorry for those who have strange tastes. That their wrong isn't theirs but the fault of their birth, and that none of us can choose our sexual tastes any more than we can account for being attractive or downright ordinary. His views were far ahead of his time, and I imagine they are still. Imprisonment had brought him face to face with a tyrannical barbarity. If there was anything calculated to stimulate his temper it was the notion of an oppressor. Powerless and therefore doubly vulnerable, suddenly deprived of all one's habits, exposed to a way of life irreconcilable with sensitivity, he claimed that the system created criminals, and that frustrated tigers tore at the legs of society on their release from behind bars. It was when he was alone at night, walking the edge of the stage in the private theatre, that he would give voice to his sufferings, most often in a loud, declamatory, monomaniacal rant. It was as though someone else spoke through him, and his breath attempted to modulate the dialogue. When he let it go he whistled like a man shaken by fever.

What I tell you comes in the random snatches that memory dictates. I've never got close to anyone in life. Most of the time I've read people more for their looks than their ability to think. I never knew my father. I was given the name Philippe, because it was that of my mother's father. When I was old enough to distinguish a predominant passion from the meaningless, diverse ways in which I expressed myself, I realized that I wanted to create images of people. I found myself concerned with items of dress: a man's tie, a woman's belt, the buttons on a jacket, the cut of a sleeve. I would draw these, paying attention to the inventive detail with which I embellished my models. I drew from pictures in books, catalogues, and eventually from my imagination. My mother was at a loss to know how I conceived of my originals. 'You can't have thought that up,' she would say. But I had. And then I would colour my creations. A bright pink jacket with a black shirt, an ivory suit worn with a matelot's striped T-shirt, a leather belt with a full moon as a clasp, a scarlet bolero on a naked body, hooped earrings that threatened to touch the waist. My improvisations were always aimed at the sensational. I drew women in white bikinis with shoulder-length black gloves and then reversed the image for men. My model wore black silk briefs and long white gloves. I worked on a drawing-board and longed to have an atelier. My clients at first were friends aspiring to create a presence in the world, young men and girls who hoped to invent a state of dress which corresponded to their inner realizations. I made little black cocktail dresses out of sequins; leotards for my camp friends; lingerie dictated by a catalogue of male fetishes; rakish hats for a stage performer; and above all whatever I cut was new, inventive, designed to attract entrepreneurial attention.

When I wasn't working I spent my time waiting for the perfect stranger to appear. That's what took me out to bars. There was suspense each time the door opened and someone crossed the floor. Would he be the one? Would my life open out into a fiction at the exchange of a glance? I think myth begins like that. The old story is renewed because there is no other. The attraction of opposites, the meeting of the same, it's all one. What we're seeking is to live by duality. A part of me wants to exist in someone else's mind, to stand out clear in their thoughts like a red sail against a blue sky, and correspondingly I want to translate that person into my nerves, learn them like a foreign language which in time grows into fluent expression. I can be me or him; I can walk him down the street naked or clothed in my mind, whip him with flowers or throw a black thundercloud of rage at his image.

It's time that I don't understand. What century am I in? The château at La Coste, that was a reality – I can still trace the outline of a scar ridged into my left buttock. And these fashion photographs? They were done by Man Ray, who celebrated the other one's algolagnia. I've learnt so much from his models. His notion of lipstick or 'the red badge of courage' as he called it, that intimate scarlet, maroon or orange insignia which is both a woman's erotic seal and her concessionary gesture to the clown, the puppet, the mime, the mask which is preferable to external features.

What time is it? I have three clocks in my studio. One points to green digital figures: 18.4.1772; another illuminates the date as 23.5.1935; and still another disagrees – it is 18.4.1992. Who am I to tell? Like the man who took me to La Coste, I have lived through so much. I have brought lilacs home in the April rain; I have found letters of objurgation left by my bed from lovers who have rifled my flat and gone; I have found my name written by an invisible presence. The Only One.

I work at my drawing-board most mornings. Man Ray was lucky, for Coco Chanel, Schiaparelli, Poiret and Worth were audacious in a way that it's impossible to be now without recycling permutations of their original designs. And Lee Miller, Meret Oppenheim, Nancy Cunard, Nusch Eluard, Peggy Guggenheim, they were models whose inimitable characteristics, the white face and dark lipstick bow, the pencil-drawn eyebrows, the cigarette elongated by a holder, maximized on the style, the flagrant mystique and smouldering vivacity of the *femme fatale*. And these women can be moved around in time. They wore kohl and jade anklets for the pharaohs, three times their body weight of satin for French eighteenth-century society, and for Man Ray's contemporaries, the weightless shadow of a silk stocking, the clear aquamarine chiffon of a négligé. All fashion is dictated by fetish. Clothes create the fantasy which the nude rarely embodies. And so I create with that in mind, abstracting the perfect figure, realizing its completion through transpicuous provocation: a woman with gold sequins for eyebrows, a cigarette angled from purple lips, a cellophane skirt sitting on her bottom like a transparent peach skin. Or my male model poses in a leather cap, a studded neck-choker, black rubber shorts with two cut-outs through which flower-shaped areas of the buttocks show. On all my models, male and female, the toenails are painted alternately black and gold.

On the day I went to La Coste, the hay-coloured late-summer light had blown over into rain. I wasn't going anywhere that day. But I was desperate for something I couldn't name. It was as though all my nerves had come to the surface of my skin – the electric points jabbing for recognition. He was just sitting there, reading, writing, making himself the centre of attraction by his indifference. And I was imagining ways in which to shock him. The lipstick I would pull from my pocket and apply to his lips, how I would travesty his aristocratic demeanour, the essentially pusillanimous disposition by which he gave the appearance of sobriety and nurtured outrage. Who was this man? I had to get to the bottom of him. He wasn't the person I had dreamt of who would write me long letters in green ink, send me flavoured teas from Mariage Frères at 13 rue des Grand-Augustins, or bring me a Patou perfume wrapped in black crêpe paper with a purple ribbon.   _

I sat down at his table, one hand angled on my hip, my manner without deference, taken up with the assertion of youth as an independent right, a blond apotheosis mirrored by the blue glass of an autumn lake. I didn't think he was going to speak. But I could sense in him a whole spatial architecture, an intricate maze of things known and explored that receded to a point with which even he had lost contact.

'Philippe?' He wanted to know my place of birth, my upbringing, where I lived now. Did I have parents? Had I run away from home? For all his implacable hauteur there was a nervousness underlying his speech. He was like a man who having been found out in his guilt had resolved to address his need by exaggerating his caution. I noticed that even while drinking he never withdrew the grey silk glove which moulded his hand. There was a fastidiousness about this man – and I have known so many bizarre traits of behaviour – which expressed itself through an extreme self-indulgence, a dissociation from any horror he perpetrated by a denial of involvement. He would always be the watcher, the man observing the act he committed with a detachment which diminished its reality. And you are probably questioning whether my degree of perception was spontaneous or has been enhanced by retrospect. What time is it?

That day belonged to no time. He said it might prove his last visit to the city before he took up what he called his customary preoccupations at the onset of autumn. He said to me: 'I shall present you with great truths; people will listen and give thought to them. Though some will meet with opposition, some at least will remain. You will find I shall have contributed in some way to psychological progress.' I remember that, and how the light was dipping blue and grey outside, the squally sky periodically building to an impasto turbulence. I knew he wanted me to join him in whatever journey he was undertaking. He assured me I might, if I wished, only be away from Paris for a weekend; his chauffeur would return me to the city. And his anticipation of my probable anxiety concurred with my own apprehensions. I had clients. I was in the process of cutting a velvet bolero, shaping a gold cabaret hat, putting together the innovative costumes that people had begun to order.

There are moments into which we enter so fully that we participate in consciousness. My decision to go stood out as a break in the time-film, a pause in which the reel momentarily stood still. I was draping my black leather jacket over my shoulders, letting it hang with my own innate sense of style, and I was taking in the bar mirror, the light as it journeyed to the centre of the room, the lonely, bluesy saxophone issuing from the record, the voice entering as still another register of pain, and all the time I was conscious of having immobilized the present. The scene would come back to me again and again. Who am I? Someone walking out of a bar, pursued by the imaginary music which accompanies any big decision.

And of course the car was waiting. It was polished to a beetle's blue-black sheen. You could have made up your face in the reflection.

I wasn't so much frightened as observant of the man who had instigated my decision to leave the capital. His eye was voracious to take in everything. Nothing escaped his vision. He was like someone who having been confined in a cage was now set upon discovering visual minutiae, the spiral zigzag of a hair arrested on my shirt, the brilliant pigment in a swallow-tail butterfly's wing occurring as the splashed motif on a woman's umbrella. His gloved hands were interlocked in the shape of a praying mantis. The contact of silk with his flesh seemed to excite him endlessly. Even his hands were engaged in creating sexual configurations, a bizarre geometry of attempted unities and deliberate malformations. Despite his apparent reserve as he sat with his head cradled at a slant into the red leather upholstery, he had as many eyes as the ocelli in a peacock's tail. Later on he was to tell me that his clearest vision came through his penis, that blind eye which he had trained to see clearly in the darkest passages.

At first he hardly spoke. He mentioned a house the other side of the river, somewhere near the Luxembourg Gardens. We wouldn't be stopping there; he was anxious to get clear of the city, to find the hectic shock of red and yellow woods efflorescing in their dying moult, to be free of cops, oligarchies, informers. With the champagne still alive in my head, and the comfort of the car nurturing my gravitation towards luxury, I found myself fantasizing about the possibilities of a relationship with this outlawed, solitary individual. I felt sure he wasn't what he was made out to be. He had been judged in human terms as being inhuman. He was a man conscious that his sexual propensities were something rare. His actions contained a future which only he could realize for others. His body was an instrument attuned to sexual mysticism. 'It is reasonable to make one's desires a measure of the truth', he was to write to me at a later date. He could trace his family back seven hundred years – his genes, he said, mirrored the violent course of history. Sometimes he could hear horses riding through his head, men imprecating, execrating, imploring help on their knees or challenging the purpose of the universe. Men cut down in youth or shouting out their vilifications in old age to the blankness of star-studded space.

We drove through suburbs. It was definitely 1992 most of the time, I could tell that by the clothes. There was a woman in a black leather mini-skirt and lipstick-red jacket; and there were men in denims, dark-blue or black jackets worn with pastel trousers. My attention gravitates to dress. And this man sitting beside me, arranging his thoughts in the pattern created by his fingers, was bridging the centuries. He could jump back three at the turn of a phrase. He said he had lived 'Without air, without paper, without ink, without everything in the world.' And it was still a psychic reality, this sense of merciless deprivation, relentless persecution, this paranoid response to being shadowed, watched through a spyhole, measured for a straitjacket, his knuckles bandaged after re-peated violence offered to a granite wall. The time in which one lives is irrelevant. We all aspire to an ascendant with which we never intersect. Pain is unquantifiable, so too is pleasure, and the perennial questioning of the meaning of life and death. There are certain unresolvable absolutes which allow us to skip centuries like stepping-stones ranged across a fast-flowing stream.

I had to imagine where I was going. It could be anywhere. Often, after dancing in nightclubs, joining hands and lips with men, catching out a green or a blue eye in its vulnerability, I would be driven to a house at dawn. And the reciprocation was one of trust. I never feared that things would go wrong. And I saw so many unexpected houses jump out at me, the car headlights illuminating a white façade, a flight of steps. An owl would be heard in a nearby clump of cobalt junipers.

What do I remember? Everything and nothing. Men who were searching for love, those whose mouths turned into a full-blown rose, and those who contracted, thin-lipped, obsessed by a fetish. Some wanted to be massaged in aromatic oils and kissed in a straight line from nape to ass, others wanted to be abused, denigrated in some way that conformed to their idea of self-debasement. One man for whom I had designed a wardrobe of suits had a bedroom full of male dolls. They stood out as black latex studs. Each wore a different coloured wig, the exotically dyed red or blue hair contrasting violently with the dark skin. And he had given each a name. I was introduced to Roland, Andy, Gregorio, Blond Noir, whatever designation seemed to fit the incongruous identity with which I was confronted. These were the inhabitants of his reality. Several of them wore the silk or cashmere designs I had made up for my client.

There were so many dawn encounters. I would wake up naked except for a blue silk tie strung loosely round my neck, worn to appease the fantasy of my still-sleeping partner. And I would begin work there and then, sketching designs on a pad, allowing myself to imagine the extravagant colour combinations I would introduce into the spring, summer, autumn collections of my devoted clients. I never worked in winter. I let the season go, with its austerities, its absence of colour.

After a time, I was able to calculate the precise moment at which he would speak. He punctuated the silence with an exact regularity which I found disquieting. It was as though he had been listening to his inner thoughts, clarifying their complex discourse at the expense of hearing anyone else. Was he deaf? Had his ear turned to a fossil after years of silence inside a cell? But his life, as I had heard and was to experience, was lived through his eye. He wanted to see his thoughts in the manner that he experienced sex. By seeing and by being seen.

Or did he assume I was street trash? Another pick-up in a bar, a rent-boy looking for a place to live, but disguising myself as someone connected with fashion, the arts, entertainment. I was already finding fault with his clothes. His orange silk shirt had been hand-tailored too stiffly; his dark-grey suit was equally inflexible, the cut too austere; but his silk dress-gloves provided just that touch of the feminine necessary to emphasize his concern with fetish, his interest in both sexes, because extreme sensuality usually implies a bi-sexual orientation.

I was beginning to drift, wondering whether I should have stayed behind in the city. We had to slow for a cortège; three or four black mourning cars tailed a sedate hearse. In the car closest to us, I could make out a woman in a pearl-grey suit and hat, her head bent into her gloved hand. Another woman was trying to comfort her. It was an isolated moment in someone's life, which we shouldn't have been witnesses to, one of those vignettes that impress on each of us our singular existence.

He spoke of Florence. 'When I lived there I was another person. I assumed the name of the Comte de Mazan. Our journey there was by a rough road through the foothills of the Alps, and so dangerous was the route I took as a means of eluding my pursuers, that the inhabitants of the villages swore my carriage was only the third to be seen on that road in twenty years. From there we entered Savoy, drove rapidly through that duchy and made our way into Italy. The police had followed me. I tell you that because in your life, in the bars you inhabit, the police are everywhere. Informers, decoys, plainclothes men. And I had worsened my case by my flight. We had stopped off at a farm for the night and I was afforded the sort of excessive hospitality that the poor offer a man who is clearly someone of means. What you may have heard of me completes the story. There was a blonde-haired daughter of about eighteen. I fascinated her. My eye looking into hers could stop her thinking. I tried the experiment repeatedly and this assertion of my power created in her a corresponding submissiveness. I would watch her freeze on a thought, as though a halo of ice had crystallized the concept to the exclusion of all others. And that night. . . . Why should I tell you? She had never known sex in that way. She experienced both ecstasy and revulsion. But the word was out. There wasn't time even to stop off overnight. I expected at any moment to be overtaken and arrested. So much of life is spent like that. We are hunted for an idea which is compelled to become an act. But to arrest the idea? That would demand mind-spies, psychics who could trap the conceptual image before it is stored in the memory cells. In this century Salvador Dali has advanced the theory of a brain-camera. . . .'

He was silent for a while. He must have been gauging my response to his personal obsessions. Did it really matter if I was Philippe? I could have been anyone. I don't believe he ever made love to a partner in his life. What he did was to project his fantasies on to an anonymous body. And so many of my clients were excited by dolls, robotic mannequins, the glacial sex imparted by a video.

'And what excited me most in Florence was Titian's Venus in the Medici Palace. I expatiated on the beauty of her buttocks. It is my only way of seeing a woman. From behind, as a reverse image of her procreative body. And as important to me was a wax model of a girl which could be opened up as a lesson in anatomy. You doubtless haven't read a novel called *Justine*, in which a surgeon dissects a living girl. Rodin? That is his name. The book has remained a curiosity. It's too long to engage one's undivided attention. I wrote it as a means of occupying myself, filling my days with sexual atrocities.

'No one has time to read in 1992. I have jumped three centuries to make that evaluation. And the person who writes a book lives in a very different time from that of his reader. The two can never intersect. The physical act of writing, crossing so many pages, always going to the right, can be consumed so quickly by the reading eye.

'But why bother you with this? What if I confessed to murder? Would you ask to be put out at the next set of lights? When sex is extreme, no one knows what the outcome will be. I have left scenes which resembled a pogrom. And I detect in you, Philippe, someone special. You are willing to trust me. You are on your way to La Coste, a building whose stone walls have turned the colour of blood. The château is coloured red. Can you imagine that? A scarlet house beneath the blue night sky, shooting stars developing tails and fins as they drop into the void.'

By this time I had resigned myself to our eventual destination. I kept measuring my physical strength against his. This man seemed too frail, too centred in inner discourse to be the notorious deviant whose name raged across the Paris underworld. And of those who had gone with him, none demanded payment, an anomaly amongst the rent-boys and transvestites who hung out in Pigalle. It was something to have known this man sitting opposite me. In the clubs, young men aspired to the reputation of having had sex with a beast. Had he left his mark? Were the scars of his whip-cuts permanent, did his fingertips leave ten singes on the buttocks?

A sexual mythology grows out of a need which increases in proportion to the desire which accommodates it. One permutation leads to another. I have seen men having sex in coffins, bondage rooms in which chains are wrapped around naked bodies. And this man? What he did was rumoured to be indescribable. 'The only real book is the unpublishable one,' he would tell me later. 'The book we write in our nerves and bury each night in the unconscious is the one we never externalize. What's written there would condemn each of us to a madhouse. But somehow they seem to have read parts of mine. Or I made certain chapters legible by my behaviour.'

I must have slept. It was dusk when I awoke. The headlights were playing out across the road in long white feelers. Bats whizzed across a field in which the outline of a chestnut mare could be seen, head bowed to the grass, the black mane falling like night over the stooped shadow. We could have been anywhere.

When I looked across, he was still vitally alert. His silk fingers were seeking an impossible position of rest: a cat's-cradle, a dance of two interweaving spiders. He resumed speaking as though there had never been a break in the narrative.

'Winters pursue me. I often feel that I'm hunted by creatures from the ice-age, mammoths, glacial monsters in the form of the police. The winters of my life are like a ball of black ice humming down a mountain slope towards a ravine. And in my dreams I stand on that ball. I can't disengage myself from its increasing momentum. And at the exact moment when I'm pitched vertiginously over the edge, I either wake up or find myself taking flight as a scarlet bird, a leathery reptilian bird which raises its wings in slow-motion above the precipice. If we survive a metaphoric death in a dream, we go on to live out the transformation.

'But let me get back to the significance of winter in my life. They have come and gone, those yellow autumns which found me at La Coste. And we are accelerating towards another. Speed distorts all conception of the past. I lived and I live, and you have become a part of my journey. Looking back is like trying to catch the wind in one's clenched fist. But I had style and a taste for sexual fetish which has gone unparalleled, a life I re-create each autumn.

'Another hour and we'll be at La Coste. What should I tell you? That I was raided. That they stripped my rooms as they would a hooker. Everything I stood for was deprecated, reviled, placed on public view. I was like a fish turned transparent in crystalline water. My château was smashed by looters. In a private room they discovered an elaborate frieze depicting the administration of an enema. When they rushed my bedroom you could have heard the air split along a seam like silk being torn. They got there by way of a maze, underground passages screened off by artificial doors. I had used these and mirror screens as experiments in disorientation. As you're unshockable, I know I can continue. Anyhow, what they saw were the obscene frescoes I had paid to have decorate the room. I have kept each detail, each panel in my head.

'In one panel there were no torsos, only the full spread of male and female buttocks. I wanted their erogenous zones to be disembodied and in that way I could focus on a depersonalized subject. I was at the time trying to learn to concentrate so fully on the sexual act as to eliminate all external intrusions. All the variants of sexual behaviour were depicted in those frescoes, which were annihilated by the intruders. There was a back spotted with red tadpoles of blood, the gag tying behind the head, and the androgynous figure administering the flagellation was being tickled with a peacock's feather by a third party. I will spare you the worst. What my detractors failed to realize was the artistry which goes into choreographing sex. It's like ballet or mime. One needs to be in control of inner and outer responses. I liked to paint asses. One cheek black, the other gold, a big red love heart placed on either side. My aim was to induce an ecstasy which neither partner had ever experienced. And sometimes they gave out. When I came I was someone and somewhere else. I went through the roof of my skull on an outbound journey to the stars.

'When I close my eyes I relive the intensity of the scatological paintings which so preoccupied me. You must
understand I thought of nothing but sex. And that meant
re-creating the human body to conform to my desires. Once
you assume the role of a creator you are God. The paintings
were attempts to create new sexual apertures. Someone could
be seen making love through a nostril. . . . I leave it to your
imagination.

'The Committee of Public Safety was by that time intent on
protecting those whom I had used for the purposes of experiment. You may not understand but I had to retreat further
into myself. The journey inwards was my escape. I found
there an even deeper refuge than I had known in the elabor-
ately contrived rooms at La Coste. I went so impenetrably far
I might have found myself at the centre of the earth. And
there was a silence such as I had never before realized. At that
still centre I could do anything. I knew every form of imaginative appeasement, and what I committed on an inner
plane seemed also to represent a physical reality. The confu-
sion between the two was what got me into trouble. You can
be arrested for something that happened at the interior because they convince you it occurred on a physical plane. And
once you confess to the misidentity you end up paranoid. Try
telling me what happened to you yesterday, today or a
minute ago. You'll have first of all to separate your thoughts
from your actions and under pressure this isn't always feasi-
ble. Once they had got me the wrong way up I grew frantic. I
confessed to things which had never physically happened.
Isn't it true that for many people the most satisfactory sexual
experiences are fantasies? Ask any man the history of his
sex life and much of it will have occurred through self-
gratification.

'I valued liberty above all things. One of my investigators
was called Monsieur Le Noir. You can appreciate the black
humour involved in that. And I became obsessed with numerology. My brain was programmed with a complex, compute-
rized system of numbers. I attributed almost any form of
random coincidence to the conjugation of numerals. I can still
remember whole sentences that I wrote to illustrate my for-

mula. "The connection you make between the number 13 and treachery proves that you deceived me on 13 October 1777." Or "This letter has 72 syllables corresponding with the 72 weeks of my imprisonment; it has 7 lines and 7 syllables, which are exactly the 7 months and 7 days from. . . ."

'An obsession, but more than that. My system of coding was already making a quantum leap into another century. Our century? Today I take speedometers, electric clocks on trust. I like to think the print-out of my mind is somehow meshed with this system. We're narrowing in on our destination simply by sitting here, heads cushioned in soft red leather. Today, one travels by letting go. When I was in the rat-hole of a prison cell I computed time through my awareness of inner space, and eventually the notion of a spatiotemporal relationship disappeared. I was somewhere else. I actually brutalized my fantasies. If you dream, Philippe, you may wake up experiencing a sense of helplessness. What you dreamt seemed to occur involuntarily, to happen independent of you. But I interposed between the oneiric and the real. If I entered a day- or a night-dream I woke up convulsed, exhausted, my hands still stained with blood. I had succeeded in making physical contact with my illusory victims. I wielded a bullwhip, I placed my mother-in-law in irons, I was rampant amongst a seraglio of flagellants. Bare ass after bare ass and none afforded appeasement.'

I drowsed in and out of his conversation. What was extraordinary was the degree of my receptiveness. I missed nothing and seemed to have every word he had spoken on recall. It was black outside the car. The headlights were our only contact with the road. I was wishing myself back in Paris, but at the same time I was excited by the prospect of realizing in myself areas of experience I had never encountered before. He said we had only another twenty minutes to go, and resumed his monologue.

'I've been accused of so many things. What was it Michelet said of the bloody cruelties of the Duc de Charolais? *"Il n'aimait le beau sexe qu'a l'état sanglant."* What if I did have recourse to aphrodisiacs? You've probably heard of cantharides – the supposedly aphrodisiac drug known as Spanish fly. It is an irritant to the bladder. A little of this drug concealed inside chocolates drove Marguerite Coste crazy. But not in terms of sexual desire. What she suffered was convulsions, intestinal spasms. But that was another time, another place. I was hunted. And even today burning up the road in a Mercedes I expect to be overtaken, I anticipate the noonday shadow of a poplar tree standing up from horizontal to vertical and developing a face and hands. That adversary would interrogate me for a past from which I can never dissociate myself. I was who? Donatien-Alphonse-François de Sade. I am who? Donatien-Alphonse-François de Sade. Son of the Comte de Sade, Chevalier-comte de la Coste et de Mazan, Seigneur de Saumane, Lieutenant-général pour le roi de la Haute et Basse Bresse, Bugey, Valromey et Gex. A distinction which worked both for and against me. And the tragedy is that one can never communicate one's true life. There's no one who understands. I wrote to convince myself that I existed, and I ended up questioning the validity of my identity. Who if anyone is the author of a book? I would say it is no one. At the height of my creativity, at the time of my deepest immersion in sexual fantasy, what I experienced was a feeling of dispossession. My hand walked across the page by itself. It wrote while I followed its movement with my eye. Left to right, left to right without intermission for three or four hours at a time. And that's why writing is the thing closest to insanity. There's no visible or tangible connection between the writer and his subject. The process doesn't even involve the contemplative satisfaction to be had by urinating. And in sex I didn't spare that function. I pissed into impaled rectums. . . . Nothing I can tell you will convince you either of my merits or defects.'

We had run into a hailstorm. I could hear the ice clipping the car roof. The car was shaken like a tambourine, little white globules spitting against the metal with a clipped vengeance. The staccato rap was the distraction I needed in order to shift plane. He had stopped talking, obsessively relating his life as it had been and as it was now. The car had entered a tree-lined drive, I knew this from the absence of space to left and right. What the headlights whitewashed was

63

a compact avenue of cypress and poplars. The wind must have been trapped high up in their crowns as in a net.

When the car came to a halt we were in front of the crenellated façade of a fortified château. The headlights stayed on an instant before cutting out. As we marched over the gravel I submitted voluntarily to the handcuffs I felt snap around one wrist and then bite into the other. I was letting go, surrendering my liberty as though I had always known this would be asked and expected of me.

The entrance hall smelt of the dark which clings to history. I nursed the unquestioning conviction that everything in my life had contrived to bring me here to this place which both fascinated and repelled me. My designer's eye kept filling in the sombre overtones with colour. I would have had the maids dressed in leather and chiffon, their short skirts riding high to the line of the bottom, and I would have presented the boy pages in leotards studded with rhinestones. As it was they were uniformly dressed in dancers' black tights with corresponding black tops. When they turned round I saw that the backs had been cut out of their tights exposing a series of powdered and rouged buttocks. This was a daily ritual he demanded. With the same regularity as a woman makes up her face so these boys and girls had to apply a similar attention to their asses.

I stood in the hall while de Sade knelt to kiss the cheeks of an epicene blond boy. He stayed down on his knees and apprehended a girl with tomato-red hair. He ran his tongue up and down her crack while she remained immobilized like a statue. His seraglio were clearly so conditioned to this mode of behaviour that they had assimilated it into their day-to-day routine.

I was led through corridors to my bedroom, the door of which was painted white and inscribed with an erect penis entering the voluptuous cheeks of a houri. The room had been prepared. A small green shaded lamp had been placed by a black satin bed. My change of clothes was awaiting me. I had to dress in backless tights, a silver top with de Sade's heraldic crest as a logo and silver high heels to add emphasis to my walk. I relished the idea of becoming a faggot, a tart, another creation who fitted into this man's fantasy of the Château of Silling with its sheer crags rising to the clouds. The furniture was likewise painted black. I had the weird notion that we were so high up that if I drew the curtains I would encounter clouds sauntering across the sky with the same vertiginous dip one experiences in looking out of an aircraft.

Initiates to de Sade's sexual rites wore silver and black. I was left alone to reflect on my condition. Paris seemed light years away, our journey here as unreal as the passage between childhood and the knowledge that one is an adult. A displacement had occurred. The child had become the adult in a spontaneous rush which defied time and space. I put my hands over my face and studied my features. I had to hold on to something. An angular cheekbone, a cranial ridge, the outline of my nether lip. I had to know myself before I was asked to give up everything to the collective obsession with anonymous sex.

Was I still Philippe, an up-and-coming Parisian fashion designer? Someone who would one day put leggy models on the catwalks? I who had made my way by dexterous experimentation. I who was capable of dressing a woman in three strategically placed sequins. Had I undergone the transition? Was I to be another automaton in this man's sexual circus, his parade of young hides before freaks?

There was a sheet of paper by the bed. It was headed 'Bastille, 8 March 1774'. I took it up and read.

'You know that exercise is more important to me than food. And yet here I am in a room smaller than the one I had before. I haven't space to swing a cat and I can leave only rarely to go into a narrow yard fetid with cooking smells, into which I am marched at bayonet point as if I had attempted to assassinate Louis XVI. How they make one despise great things by attaching importance to inconsequential things.'

There wasn't time to read more. A maid knocked at the door and told me I was to go with her to the hall. I felt compelled to follow. Getting there was by way of an endless maze of corridors, through which I walked like an automaton behind the bare painted bottom of a girl who might have been here for centuries. She expressed no emotion, no hint of fraternity or sorority. She walked as though the motion was performed independent of her. Occasionally a door to right or left would open and frightened eyes would show fractionally before disappearing back into the dark. Once I caught sight of a red mask, an eye with an elongated tear-drop suspended from it on a painted stem. I imagined I was on film. There was no tangible link between my past and present. Had I really travelled here voluntarily with de Sade, the notorious sexual beast who according to history was periodically imprisoned for sodomy? This man simply went in by the back entrance and stayed there too long. If he was in search of anything it was an exit from life. He might have thought to find it there, a passage to the unknown.

I was conducted into a large hall. There were leather couches, leather chairs, glass tables, several imposing chandeliers weighted with lightning-storms of crystal and an improvised stage draped with red and purple cloths. Young people sat silently on the couches. He was there occupying a narrow cane-backed chair in front of the stage. He had distributed his weight to keep almost perfect balance on the chair. He sat there oblivious of the others. Whatever his state of mind he was without doubt fixated, waiting for something he had already imagined. And once we get into this habit we are unappeasable, for reality always falls short of illusion.

I realized that I was to be led on to the stage. The lights dropped and a single white spotlight pooled itself on the boards. I knew I was positioned where so many had stood before me. I was no longer Philippe. I was someone else. I would be rechristened, initiated as an adept to sexual rites. Paris seemed so far away. Was it a dream? And my stylish apartment in the historic rue du Pot de Fer, furnished with mannequins dressed according to the dictates of my fashion, in leather caps, chains, togas? Had I dreamt my past existence and the long car ride to La Coste?

Now there was no light at all. I could hear his voice begin to intone, while fingers and tongues flickered over my body like a shoal of nervous fish.

'For, cross the bridge and you come down into a little plain

66

covering about four acres, surrounded on all sides by sheer crags rising to the clouds, peaks which enclose the plain in a faultless screen. The passage known as the bridge path serves as the sole means of communication with the plain; the bridge removed or destroyed, there is not on this entire earth a single being, of no matter what species you may imagine, capable of gaining access to this plot of level land. . . .'

His voice was growing louder as I blacked out. Before I did so I remembered an incident from my life, his, the journey here? I had been waiting in a room. I had an appointment and was apprehensive for I had forgotten the reason for my going there. I flicked through a glossy magazine, a current edition of Paris *Vogue*, but not even the extravagant fashion shots gained my attention. I was listening all the time for approaching footsteps, but was unable to prepare myself for the impending interview. I was in that state of displacement experienced sometimes on waking in a foreign place. I was disconnected. It was like waking up inside a dream but finding oneself unable to get back to reality. And perhaps that was it: I was conscious within the context of a dream. There was a scorpion on the table and I let it rest on the back of my left hand. It stayed there like a bizarre glove and started to rattle. I wasn't afraid. I continued to stare at it. And then the door opened. A man came in whom I recognized as de Sade. He was carrying his stone head in his hands, for it was too heavy to wear. I noticed that one of my silver neckties was fastened around the stone neck. I was about to ask him where he had bought it, when the whip cut my back. I stood up to the ferocity of the initial cuts, the pain sending tributaries of fire along my spine and forcing me to breathe as though I was running uphill. When I blacked out I was attempting to catch his stone head as it rolled towards the edge of a cliff. I went down into the dark in pursuit of it.

Five

It's such a long way down to the end of things, if there ever is a resolution of experience. Sometimes the iron stairs notched into a cliff-face seem to terminate in mid-air. I find myself holding on to tusks of smoke, unable to separate conscious-ness from dream, illusion from reality. And if I lost my footing, went the whole way down, would I find my ruined château on the sands, with broken windows and fire-gutted gables, surrounded by the incoming tide?

And Philippe? I have encountered so many rent-boys, the endless fragments of a city's streets, those who are rootless as seeds blown across sand and those who are looking for a father in the dictates of the whip.

I once wrote, 'I was born to be served and I would have it so.' Philippe served me by listening. In his stay at La Coste he learnt sufficient about me to write a biography. He was concealed behind the drapes when I delivered my endless monologues on the stage at night. I would pace the boards naked or draped in a heavy Russian fur, describing those parts of my ancestry I wanted to make known:

'Related, through my mother, to the most prestigious fam-ilies in the realm; attached on my father's side to everyone of distinction in the province of Languedoc; and born in Paris to great riches, I thought as soon as I could think, that nature and fortune had combined to my advantage; I declared so, because people were stupid enough to tell me, and this ridiculous prejudice made me condescending, despotic and irascible; it seemed that everyone should obey me, that the entire universe should flatter my needs, and that I alone possessed the right to conceive and satisfy such tastes.'

I acted out my part in earnest. I acquired a mystique or aura which mâde me irresistible to anyone with a flaw in their psychosexual make-up. Their curiosity about my habits led them to expose their own intimate propensities. It was as though I was walked through, as though a transparent partition allowed people to explore my interior. When they went back into the real world it was to complain of what they had seen. They externalized my fetishes, hung them up like cobras from hooks, and passers-by on the road shot bullet-holes through their livid skins. I was persecuted by those who secretly nurtured the desires I had the courage to pursue. And if they once participated in what they called my crimes, they howled for retribution, forgetting that an attraction to pleasure was what brought them to the black drapes and erotic frescoes of my flagellant's inner sanctum.

And sex for me was inextricably linked with tabulated figures. How many? What number of blows could they withstand? What was the proportion of those who disappeared either from malpractice or death? I compiled lists. One of them related to the inhabitants of the Château of Silling.

Masters	4
Elders	4
Kitchen staff	6
Storytellers	4
Fuckers	8
Little boys	8
Wives	4
Little girls	8
Total	46

Of these, thirty were immolated and sixteen returned to Paris.

FINAL ASSESSMENT

Massacred prior to 1 March, in the course of the orgies	10
Massacred after 1 March	20
Survived and came back	16
Total	46

It has never been my purpose to offer consolation, my concern is with truth. In one of my prison stays I requested a coat the colour of Parisian mud. I wanted to wear my feelings; my skin had come into contact with stone and dirt so often that I knew myself to have acquired the pigment of my surroundings. When I stood up I was like a column of earth. I could feel bits of stone and glass and bottle caps sticking to my body. And this was a way of assimilating my environs, making myself equal to the situation which grew on me like a shadow. At times the darkness in my cell would become tangible. I could place my arms around it and confront its weight with my volume. I was a column embracing another column. In that way I would stand for hours making myself equal to my opposition.

But before I return to Philippe or any of the fraternity who joined me in those long insulated winters on my estate, I want to recapitulate the agonized dilemma of my imprisonment. I was constrained but at the same time free to build in inner space. If they poked meat at me on a stick I would receive it seated on an imaginary gold chair. I might be picking the first sun-blushed orange in Seville or walking on the cratered solar dust of another planet when all the while my enemies imagined me stuck like a rat in a hole. Who am I? I am a man travelling between all times. Somehow I can't get off the road I knew first in a carriage and now in a chauffeur-driven Mercedes. For some of us there appears to be no exit from time. And my memory is infallible. I shall repeat to you part of a letter I wrote in Vincennes in 1783. I was pleading my case by enumerating diverse sexual practices sanctioned around the world. What I found myself saying has subsequently entered into the province of surrealism.

If one were to go to the King of Achem, who is attended by 700 playthings, to whom three or four hundred lashes are administered daily for the least wrong, and who tests blades on their heads, or to the Emperor of Golconda, who goes out riding on twelve women arranged in the shape of an elephant and who sacrifices twelve of them with his own hand each time a prince of the blood dies, if I were to approach these men with the tale that there is a little corner of ground in Europe where a certain Monsieür Le Noir daily pays 3,000 informers to find out how the inhabitants of that place ejaculate their sperm; and that there are prison cells waiting and death-sentences instructed for those who have not yet learnt that it is a crime to open the 'sluice' to the right rather than the left; and that the register of excitement at such a time when nature compels them to open it, and Monsieur Le Noir to keep it shut, was punished by death or twelve to fifteen years imprisonment; if, I say, someone went and told this to the various leaders, you must agree that they in their turn would have every right to shut the informer away as a madman. . . .

And I have known interiors which are worse than the most constricted padded cells. I would meditate on the eye of my penis. I had shot strings of pearls into the most sensitive of all orifices. Those pearls had grown in proportion until they became angry moons colliding with each other. Even those who had at first entered willingly into sex turned on me with unmitigated rage. What they felt was that my discharge had become a contaminated yeast which would rise and grow into a hideously deformed embryo.

The winter that Philippe came to the château was memorable for the prolonged, burnished autumn. The reds, golds, powdered coppers, the dazzling rains falling obliquely over the vines, the smell of childhood rising in the damp, the elongated lightnings which zigzagged into crazy spirals. If I could have held up my hand and left my fingerprints on the sky, that thin azure which predominated by day, I would have achieved a contact with reality that eluded me in sex, in

71

writing, in every form of human participation. Imagine it. Five white fingerprints floating over between clouds, en route for the ocean and bound for the Alps, Florida and LA. I wanted to make a tangible impression on the blue *tabula rasa*. A single moment's realization that I had existed in the great, meaningless flux.

In between devising unique geometric patterns for sex, an occupation which exhausted me mentally, I wrote my experimental plays for an absurdist theatre. When I wasn't acting out my desires physically I was projecting a shadow play, creating abstract configurations, and thinking of other plays which were to involve dolls, those most submissive of all sexual partners. I could hear my voice return to me as though it came from another area of my brain. Right to left, left to right with spontaneous co-ordination. There's a theory that schizophrenia arises from inheriting the instructive oracular deity in the wrong brain hemisphere. The voice rooted in primal origins is inexhaustible in the dialogue it maintains. It goes back to the roots of speech and beyond that to a pre-verbal interpretation of the universe. I was so often in touch with that source that I took it to be natural. How else can a theatre be established? Voices arrive in the head and go out on to the page. They become a reality, as Philippe was a reality, and the prison cells that I tried to enlarge by pushing my weight against the obduracy of stone. I could never dissociate sex from any human activity. It impregnated everything I did. In me it was like fire running through dead bracken. I would be sitting writing, thinking, meditating on the occult significance of numbers, or just staring at a log breaking into blue and green flames, and all the time I would be distracted, obsessed by erotic fantasies.

Philippe was useful to me, not only in terms of sexual practice but in his ability to design clothes and screens for my theatre. He was adept at sketching out my fetishistic proclivities. The leather face-masks, studded basques, neck-chokers, shorts, micro-skirts, anklets, the whole S&M inventory that lived in my mind. Or I would have him work at screens. I wanted scatological extravaganzas. And Philippe executed these in the livid colours he had come to use in fashion. A

series of thirty or forty asses lifted in the air might be offset
against a silver or orange background. And sometimes he
used fabrics for the screens. Leather or silk. I would order his
materials to be delivered to the château: a riot of sensuous
textures to be violated by the impression of wounded organs.
At one time I had attempted to write for a populist theatre.
But seeing my work rejected, considered unfit for audience
consumption, I turned towards a private expression aimed at
giving voice to my intrinsic preoccupations. My unpublished
plays are numberless. *Les Jumelles ou le choix difficile*, *Le
Prévaricateur ou le magistrat du temps passé*, *L'Ecole des
jaloux ou la folle épreuve*, *La Tour mystérieuse*, *Les Fêtes de
l'amitié*, I could name so many. They have become the con-
jectural suppositions of bibliographers. Unpublished works,
improvised, unknown because I acted them out with a select
company of sexual initiates. What Philippe had was the ability
to live in a state of auto-suggestion. I had tried this with all of
those who visited the château. I wanted the receptive consciousness of somnambulists to infuse all my subjects, so that
at the slightest hint they would prove receptive to my dictates. My dream was to enter the anacoustic zone and to
function with a mute seraglio. Perhaps I should have ordered
the extraction of tongues on immediate entry to La Coste.

There was a fragment, a short play I wrote, a mini-drama,
more filmic than made for the stage. I'm going to resketch it
as best I can.

The theatre is in darkness. A figure enters from behind the
audience. His naked body is sprayed iridescent gold. He
walks along the aisle, carrying a black mask. When he reaches
the stage, he puts on the mask out of which two intensely
bright lights shine. One is the sun and the other the moon. He
crouches and lights candles. Now we can see ten silver sacks
hanging from the ceiling. Music suggests funerary rites. As we
watch, the sacks begin to scream. The central figure takes a
whip and gives each of them a resounding cut. He kisses the
whip-handle and places his instrument of correction in front
of a mirror which serves as an altar. He kneels and performs
imprecations before the mirror.

When he rises, he cuts down the suspended sacks. Two

assistants come on stage and help him with his task. They line up the sacks and cut them open. Out of each, a figure crawls. Five are men and five are women. They are dressed in black transparent body-stockings. They are wearing scarlet lipstick and heavy theatrical make-up. They proceed to run rapidly round a white circle painted on the stage. They are like frightened horses in a corral.

The gold figure stands in the centre of their circle. He places the whip between his legs and bows. He addresses the eye of his erect penis. He faces the audience and draws a red lipstick circle on his helmeted cock.

> *Gold Figure*: I am empty of all human emotion. My concern is with pleasure.
> *Echo*: You have cut your heart out and left it beating in a black box.
> *Gold Figure*: I buried that box. I would have the weight of the Bastille sit on it. May it never be found. What I have cultivated is desire.
> My eye and my genitals.
> *Echo*: You have developed a satanic satyriasis. To you it is the only expression of reality.
> *Gold Figure*: May I never repent. Never. Never.
> NEVER.

As his voice dies away so a single white spotlight picks out the figures on stage. A red light dissects the white cone. The ten figures present their asses to the gold figure, and on each is written a series of numerals. The gold figure releases a snake from a basket and coaxes it, allowing it to ravel its coils around his arm and shoulder. His left cheek tilts to caress its head. The tongue of the snake flickers in darting, inquisitive jabs across his flesh. In response to the snake's phallic mimicry, the man plays sensitive fingerstops on his erect penis. While the ten figures are still bending over he releases the snake, which alerts itself to their presence. The man ties on a ritual black blindfold. The snake zigzags in slow capricious coils towards the two figures to the far left. Unconscious of the threat, they remain arched in a posture of submission.

Their wrists are chained. All of them, male and female, wear scarlet stilettos. They are balanced on brittle wine-glass stems. As the snake makes its reconnaissance, so the strobe-lights grow more frenetic. Red and white lightnings intersect with green and violet rays. The scene fades out with the shriek of someone conjecturally bitten by the snake's fangs, and the sound of savage whip thrusts raked across the passive victims.

I remember. And memory is a series of codified cells, the acquisition of images numbered like a film strip. Ilford 18a. Somewhere in the electronically stimulated archives which constitute my impressions of a lifetime, several lives, the fluid extension into omnipotent consciousness, are incidents, particulars which accuse me of having lived. In each of us there are characteristics which serve as fixed stars: what I did, who I was, what I do, who I am. Sometimes I could scream to be free of consciousness.

There were things that happened each time I locked the gates of the château and entered that state of discourse with my sexual energies that led to psychotic revolt, pathological turbulence, that burned me, remaining like viruses, recurring cyclically with shadow symptoms. I am a mind through which every perversity orbits. And I am someone who finds beauty in everything. Even staring at the muddiest prison latrine I can see the surface dance with emeralds, sapphires, chalcedonies. I have seen a petrified forest inside an interrogation cell, I have retrieved hummingbirds from blood spilt in the street, I have watched gold wings extend from the shoulders of someone whom my whip-hand has reduced to a series of blue and purple pulped horizontals.

There was always this intrusion. If it wasn't the law, it was the paranoid suspicion that there was an eye staring at me from a corner, a bright lens superimposed on the tenuous strata of light, or else watching me from the sky. A white eye at noon and a red eye at midnight. Or it was a shadow, something poking in intrusively, flat to the ground like a snake's belly, occupying the gaps between my thoughts, hissing through the vacant silence in which we live when we are focused on nothing, no image, no disturbance of being.

And perhaps the nature of crime lies in being found out,

not by anyone in particular, but by the shadow. There's someone inside us who makes a long journey through labyrinthine corridors, through galaxies of dead brain cells, DNA spirals, genetic blueprints, to arrive as an arresting voice in the consciousness. We don't even know who or what it is. I was never free from it. Only in the liberating moment of orgasm was my double temporarily obliterated. Sex is a series of blizzards: the white storm obscures everything but the image of its desire. In those ecstatic, highwire jabs I achieved vision. I was a cosmonaut, a traveller through galaxies. I had created supernovas, I followed the volcanic lava of my ejaculation to its last fractional release. I burnt in the luminous cone described by its orbit. A series of in-focus asses came in so close that I brought them right into my mind. If thought can establish the contact of touch, then my fantasy explored a sensory tactility. I aimed to violate, force myself on the images which streamed across my mind. I wanted to slash holes in my brain, so damage my conjurations that when they returned they would be unrecognizably distorted, a reversed cycle of casualties imploring that I continue to mutilate them.

And there was the other side to me. I would place scarlet roses by my bed and stare at them, apprehend their beauty, the involuted turban expanding outwards in concentric dilations, pushing towards limits, but never letting go of the secret eye contained at the centre. A petrified red hurricane compact on a stem. Later on I would take those roses outside, and one by one trample them into the mud, into ruts left by a skidding tyre. Beauty always drove me to breaking point. And having defiled petals, rich fabrics, books on which the craftsman had set a gold seal, I would relish their value the more under the heel of my boot, stamping them into a puddle, realizing the momentary apotheosis they took on in their disfigurement.

What do I want? What does any of us hope to find? Ultimates are often retrieved from the underworld. I have smelt the fragrance of lily-of-the-valley in a fetid prison cell. I have seen precious stones blaze across a blank concrete wall. I have known valleys of tropical fauna shine out in the sphincter I was about to penetrate. Horses knelt in the grass. Someone played a piano buried behind a green curtain of orchids and lianas. And I was suffocated. I had to unleash my fury in order to break through the soporific illusion. I had to tear grass out by the roots, storm the interior like a tornado crashing over a continent. When I withdrew I was someone else. I belonged to another species, a race of mutants travelling in saucers from one planet to another.

Sex and theatre. They are intimately related. I wanted to conflate the two, make them interchangeable. My aim was to establish perpetual motion. I wrote plays in which the action was continuous, in which the dressing-rooms were also the stage, so that the action was one of constant exposure, a multiplication of planes which allowed no privacy. And my sexual habits demanded the same unremitting histrionics. As long as I could perform I wanted an audience. The thrill was meaningless to me unless I was being watched. Someone else had vicariously to experience my pleasure and perhaps maximize on it for me to achieve orgasm. In that way I was cloned. If I turned around I could see myself multiplied into a generative line of robotic automata. Endless duplications of myself, figures on the time screen we come to call memory. There were so many of me that I disputed the claim that I was guilty of sexual crimes. There was de Sade ABCDEFG. When the chain bit into my wrist it could have been anyone's, that ugly red and purple contusion of my flesh. I would be dragged like an animal into a cell for charges that seemed unaccountable to my inner freedom. And will there ever be an end to it, the irreconcilable conflict between what happens on the mental and on the physical plane?

It's always autumn in my inspiration. Lyricism is touched by red and gold, the Septembering of trees, the ripening of the vine, the wine that spills into one's chemistry. The imprint of fermented sunlight on the senses. There were days inside the confinement of stone when the smell of damp leaves lifted from the floor with the palpable force of a blow. I wanted to scoop up armfuls of tan and umber and vermilion leaves, hold their cool to my face, splash them like stencils over my body. There are so many springs, summers, winters – they pursue their individual cycles, but autumn stays. It is the realization of all the things we will never be. It traps memory in a glass. A gold stag comes out of the forest to greet us on the road, the love we knew in youth is there again, a hand waving from the city's highest stair. If it's a woman she throws her white dress down at our feet. If it's a man he takes off his shirt and has it kite slowly downwards into our uplifted hands. At the nuclear core of creativity everything is fluid, time no longer exists. I'm here and now and everywhere within the progress of the line. The written word encapsulates the quality of semantic DNA. I can implant a lifetime's experience into a phrase, an image. A single word can resonate with aeons of genetic inheritance.

Philippe understood to an extraordinary degree the tenuously interchangeable relationship between victor and victim. When I punished him I was punished. My pleasure came from relaying his pain to my nerves. In that way my action established a duality. It was I who was experiencing the force of my whip-hand, that's why I went to such extremes. I could believe that my partner felt nothing. If there was blood it was mine. I was shocked at how little he felt. My tolerance to pain had grown, so I had to enter an orgasmic frenzy to stimulate my jaded nerves.

There are days in which I wonder how this happened to me, what lived in me, programmed me to demand such extremes of desire. Then there was the elaborate caution which was a condition of my enterprise, and the constant expenditure involved in arranging for my life to be lived at the centre of a sexual theatre. I needed omnipotence, a lion-tamer's control. There were times when my company came to me dressed in animal skins as leopards, zebras, tigers. They would cross the floor on all fours to symbolize bestiality. I would lead them through a maze of corridors on collars and chains, a tiger in my right hand, a leopard in my left. And there was only one route – the way that led to my secret room. Today I would have used wall-to-wall video screens to record my actions. And perhaps my writing would have lacked the intensity that comes from re-creating something through memory. What I did or did not do has become the subject of contemporary myth. My sexual propensities have grown to be an underworld inheritance. The young man with a shaved head hanging in chains has found me alive in his genes. I am the psychic valency in his testosterone. And the young-woman dressed in thigh-high latex boots has inherited my obsession. She is my feminine impersonator. Unable to be lashed by me, her vicarious orgasm is generated by her partner's ecstatic suffering.

I am a molecular cosmonaut. A traveller between worlds. On the day that I made love to Philippe, de Chirico might have conceived his white horses – the ferocity of my discharge created the formative genes of a new species. Philippe? He was the clothes designer, the young man we drove from Paris to La Coste. His body was no different from the five thousand with whom I had experimented. I remember him why? Because emotions are an interchange of neurons? Or because the vague hint of vanilla on his breath recalled spring, the pink and white hawthorns, purple tusks of lilac grazing the cheek as one ducked under bushes, tiger-coloured wallflowers raising an exuberant scent that could split the nostrils like new-mown grass. Philippe was a part of that sensory amalgamation by which I lived. Where is he now? He might be hanging out in a gay bar or dead, awaiting reincarnation. And if he returns he will be a hairdresser, a designer, someone whose hair dye is a new expression of art.

In 1784 I wrote to my wife about the symptoms attendant on an infection of the prostato-urinary tract. I described my sexual anomaly. I gave voice to a viral defect. Honesty was always a part of my life, my lives. Ejaculation had become intensely painful and unpleasant, and I needed to implant my fear. My wife was the one correspondent in whom I felt an ambivalent sense of trust and betrayal. It didn't matter to me if my condition became known – in that case it would enter the slipstream of history.

> It resembles an epileptic fit – and if I did not adopt
> tedious precautions, I'm sure they would suspect as
> much in the Faubourg Saint-Antoine, from my
> convulsions, spasms and pain – you saw what it was like
> at La Coste – and if it's anything, it's twice as bad, so

judge accordingly. . . . I've tried to analyze what brings on this fit and my only clue lies in the extreme thickness – as if I was trying to squeeze cream through a narrow-necked flask. This granular secretion makes the blood vessels swell up and tears them. What am I to do?

There are times when our physical responses are tested by abnormal functioning. I found myself with a solidified volcano. My desire was constant, but I feared to release it. The imbalance in my nerves was a cosmic upheaval, a physiological mutation which threatened me with madness. I who had founded my life on my orgasmic trajectory was suddenly and pathologically constrained. It was like the earth had stopped breathing through its pores. And there was no medicine to alleviate my condition. I equated my illness with monstrosity; teratological horns, fins and flippers had begun to spawn in my testes. My keeper would find the cell littered with toads, salamanders, viscous saurians. Snakes would flick across the stone floor, gold and green lightnings zigzagging for an exit.

Out of this pain, this real and asphyxiating physical immurement in which I suffered, I wrote. There could have been no other form of expression. Like Jean Genet I found myself inhabiting a psychophysical microcosm. My sight, my lungs and my senses were ruined. I neither wanted to be inside nor out there in the world which once I had relished. There comes a point beyond which the senses cannot extend. My nerves went dead as though anaesthetized. It was like feeling with frozen fingers, eating with a tongue insensitive to taste, smelling with no olfactory response, getting aroused but having the fantasy escape to nothing. A block-shaped figure: square, eyeless head, square torso, square breasts, square legs, square feet. Just a chunk out of the Bastille stone which confronted me, and on which I would rub my face, testing it as a cat might arch its back against a tree. At times I wore stone gloves. My feet were granite, my head was a monolithic cube.

But at La Coste I was fluid. My senses were enflamed. Even the finest silk was too coarse to my touch. I would have my empty bath filled with heavy crimson rose petals and luxuriate in their voluptuous contact with my skin.

I was living to overtake my age. This is still my concern.
Somewhere in the abstract configuration of future bodies,
mutant geometries, I will find release. And I wrote to project
that future. I would speak to Philippe, to myself, to nothing. I
would declaim the visions which lived in the black book
buried at the centre of the earth. There are always those who
have access to this text. They read it in dreams, discover it in
hallucinogens, decipher it while sleep-walking through phar-
aonic tombs, pillars of white silk, through landscapes that
give on to a rectangle in space. There's a floating chair and
table, white against the azure sky. The black book is spread
open on the suspended table-top. In it I read:

> In the beginning the sky was square. The planets were
>   cubes.
> There was an alphabet in the stars. It read de Sade.
> Those letters procreated. They formed temporal
>   constellations.
> Insanity lived in a house. It was called La Coste.
> Mania was tubular. It became a phallic obelisk.
> Its force was a hurricane. A circular apocalypse.
> Omnipotence means mastery. Of all the senses.
> Ejaculation is knowledge. Of primal cosmogony.

Didn't I shout my discovery to the empty theatre? To the
blackness which was just a void without the intrusion of a
spotlight. I was arrested by my own power. In the silence of
this stone house I imagined I was god. I had created a new
species. They offered me their scars in return for the pain I
had inflicted. I imagined there was a deep pit at the centre of
the house. There were white horses trapped in that vortex.
Dreams took shape there in the way that one watches cloud
formations build to a vaporous roof above a blue bay. I have
seen clouds like a herd of white elephants in the sky above
Paris. At La Coste the dream-cumuli were tempestuous black
thunderheads. If I had dispersed these creations uniformly
about the universe, it would have meant an end to life. Continents would have rioted; insurrections would have resulted in

immediate genocide. I had to constrain my potential. I looked into the evolutive maelstrom and stood a long time in contemplation. Every possibility presented itself. I saw dictators shouting from rostrums, remonstrating, demanding over microphones. I saw them collapse backstage in bullet-proof dressing-rooms, a doctor carefully injecting minims of adrenalin into their tired hearts. And there was flame, the heat-flash which would surprise the universe. I came back to this place night after night and when I turned away, I was like someone paralysed by shock. I spent hours, days, weeks searching for my room in the maze of corridors. What I was carrying with me was the weight of the future. Even my victims couldn't succeed in waking me from this trance. I was walled in by my own imaginative findings.

Names came back to me: my wife's, Renée-Pélagie de Montreuil, those of Rose Keller, Jeanne Testard, my mother-in-law and principal antagonist Madame de Montreuil, a string of sexual acquaintances. I was ill. In my dream a blue dog came to me carrying an oval mirrored tray. When I looked for my image it was a stalk-eyed insect I saw waving its antennae at the glass, with big protuberant eyes, a fat body encased in a black armour-plated shell. For a whole week I lived in dread of that messenger returning from the underworld. I lived with my curtains drawn. Even the echo of a footstep in some other part of the house sounded like the abrupt sonic crack that precipitates a landslide. My nerves ran across the surface of my skin. I had visited those places that are sovereign to madness. Black and red and green suns had rolled along the skyline. I had seen a species emerge from nuclear dug-outs so changed by shock that they had turned into pin-thin radioactive psychotics, a man and woman walking out under the sky to bury their children in the absolute silence of dust. I saw the concourse of earth with sky, and there was not a bird, not a wind travelling through the vacuum. The man was so thin that if a fly had existed it would have knocked him over.

And slowly I got better. The room stabilized. I admitted the light into my day. The late autumn crowded its last red and gold effusion of dank leaf into my vision. My desire returned. I would avoid that pit at the centre of the night, at the centre of my life.

Can you understand, you who read this in whatever century you belong, that I acted constantly under the threat of arrest? Whatever I did in my interludes of freedom took on the expansion of timelessness. An action embodied a delayed transition between inner and outer worlds. It may have belonged to one or the other or both. What we do is most often what we remember. But there's another form of doing, involving what we forget or unconsciously choose to eliminate from memory. And when we discover the missing links in our lives, the connections stand out like blood spots on a white tile. I did that yesterday, last year, or three centuries ago?

In prison I learnt what I had forgotten. This was the real punishment. There is so much that goes missing in our lives that we assume it will no longer have a purchase on us. But images return with the sort of visual distortion that makes one think of a camera fed on LSD. Inner space detonates with technicolour implosions. All catastrophes, wars, mutilations, tortures streamed through my head and then the scene would slow to a single, isolated image, an act I had committed. Only it would be transposed in time and place. Some error on my part in childhood, some acute embarrassment surrounding a breach of côurt etiquette, would be re-enacted in a Spanish courtyard, a Florentine brothel, a yard in which an emaciated child sat on a red cushion smoking a hookah. These imaginary places had become the precincts associated with events quite foreign to them.

There was and still is the rumour that I was mad. There are those who attribute my sexual tastes to insanity. I, Donatien-Alphonse-François de Sade, am conceived as psychotic, obsessed, a man who invented every form of physical and sexual torture, whose writings germinated the seed for the Psychopathia Sexualis, and who crawled around a stone cell, myopic, racked with pain, but cradling a black snake in my hands which I would swallow if interrupted and then have rematerialize from an aperture in my spinal column.

I who have picked lice from my body in impoverished rooms in the Place Vendôme and the Section des Piques, who have been denounced as an aristocrat and counter-revolutionary when the guillotine worked night and day in Paris, its abrupt swish dislodging the head into a basket, have watched over time, over changing epochs. Wasn't I living in an apartment in the rue de Rivoli when the Reichstag unfurled its red flags, and a black sun in the form of a swastika rose over Europe? And didn't I sit at the feet of Aleister Crowley at the Abbey of Thelema in Sicily? There I met the Scarlet Woman and was instructed in the symbolism of zoosexual esotericism. The dog for the anal zone, the scorpion for genitalia, the monkey for the hands, the snake for the tongue, and the owl for the faculty of occult vision. And wasn't I somewhere else a tycoon, a mogul, always someone adopting a mask to conceal their true identity?

With Philippe it was different. I was able to jump from the past to the present without having to conceal facets of either. I had lived, I live, and fundamental character traits never alter. No genetic permutations could effect a change in my psychosexual orientation. Shut off behind the blue tinted windows of my Mercedes, driven through a modern city at night, or overtaking cars on a clear stretch of road bordered by pines, heading south for the coast, I am still conscious of my exceptional ancestry, my title and the ineffable loneliness which has always accompanied me. Solitude sits on my knee like a blue cube cut out of the sky. If I kept a pet it would be a cloud smelling of the big open spaces, of rain falling across savannahs and prairies, sheeting into the Pacific.

When I'm not at La Coste I travel. I hallucinate episodes from my past. One day walking up a sand-hill, I encountered my father, that old grand seigneur, restrained and unfalteringly formal. When he died he left nothing behind him but inalienable land and debts. He had been an ambassador in Russia and later in London. He was cold like the underside of a stone. His extravagance was unaccountable. The man burnt money in foreign countries; it was dissipated with the prodigality of someone dependent on cocaine. When I came up the crumbling dune he was standing there, left profile turned towards the aquamarine skyline. He was holding something in his right hand, his eyes fractionally averted from encountering the object. As I drew closer, I realized that it was the statuette of a naked woman, only there was a hole right through her heart. My father's frigid hauteur, his arrogant condescension, had destroyed her. The figure was composed of ash. I inhaled deeply and blew it away in a snowstorm of grey particles. And at the same time my father dematerialized. Nothing remained of him but a heart-shaped stone. I pocketed the object. I still have it. Somehow we were all turned to stone: my father, my mother, my wife, her relatives, my body during the years of imprisonment. And perhaps part of my obsession, my permanent sexual rage, was aimed at becoming flesh. My penis was hard, lithic. I had to defuse its potential, no matter that in doing so I earned for myself the contemporary sobriquet of 'The Divine Marquis'. I who converted money into flesh and flesh into a ritualized and bloody pogrom. What was I looking for? The transmogrification of my partner into a third sex, an android, a species containing ten senses and a deathless body. When I stood back from what I had done, contemplated the fresco of welts, the prostrate, quivering person I had flayed in my state of ecstatic trance, I was expecting to see their transformation. I imagined them confronting me, a gold figure extending a silver hand to offer me a scarlet rose. And they would deny me the corresponding change. I would remain rooted in flesh. My ulcerated hand would show nothing but the imprint of a whip-handle, a speckled ridge banded across my palm.

The one city I would never revisit is Marseilles. I knew I could never relive my findings there. The smell of the port, wet hawsers creaking on the tide, sailors searching the streets like wolves, women waiting outside doorways, a room-key in one hand, a lazy cigarette drooping from a scarlet lip. Orders had been served on me at one time to keep away from the city for three years. My conviction was later quashed as 'erroné et vicieux de forme' and my sentence transmuted to a heavy fine. But my enemies were implacable. I was pursued. Even when asleep I would see eyes watching in the back of my head, my dreams would lead me into alleys. They would be waiting, dressed in greatcoats and lowered hats. The place was an *impasse*. The one I faced would be mirrored by the one behind. They would shoot simultaneously, the two bullets intersecting in the middle of my skull.

And here I am recounting this in the sober daylight, the January sky blackened by rooks overhead, my two hands at rest on my right knee, the world as curious as it is voluminous.

There was a time when I was moved to four prisons in ten months. The last of the four comprised an elegant town house, a cultivated garden and, because I was no longer confined to a cell, the society of women. And then the execution site was moved to a spot right beneath our windows. The garden became a cemetery, and I as a prisoner buried eight hundred people, of which one-third came from our house. I was to have been guillotined on 11 November, but the previous day the blade sliced off Robespierre's head.

It was a time of terror. I have always been fastidious about my hands, about the velvet gloves I have worn. I was forced to dig these headless corpses into a deep pit cut into the lawn, around which topiary had created a formal garden. There were winter shrubs, late roses maintaining their stiff, white involutions. I was an aesthete transformed into a gang labourer, I who even with the most attenuated findings of my palate had compared the taste of excrement to that of an olive. I revolted inwardly against the touch of things foreign to my body. Those rain-smudged, grey November afternoons, the ululation of the bloodthirsty Paris mob resonating as a circular backdrop of sound in the lowered sky, the whole collective dementia running like a tidal wave over the city's roofs, when with my body made transparent by fear, I grew to be acquainted with death and the dead. I began to attach numerals to my interments, and in that way I came to dehumanize, depersonify the bodies heaped at my aristocratic feet. A crazy schema of numbers streamed through my mind, huge, close up like enquiring planets. Code-systems, serials, algebraic formulae, figures which bleeped like red pulsars, my head was jammed with cabbalistic equations.

Today, I lean back and codify the digits on my car-phone. I wait for a voice to answer me in Amsterdam, Copenhagen, New York. An affirmative or negative tone. I want something. I have always been in need. Desire can never be fulfilled. Sometimes I dial and don't speak. I know that I want the inexpressible, the unattainable, the ultimate enigma which can never be appeased. So I keep on travelling. Speed is a narcotic, landscapes break up like planes in an abstract painting, the road has no beginning and no end. I have no beginning and no end.

Interrogate a man and what you find at his interior is a stranger. A monkey sitting on an ironing-board, a mannequin divested of its clothes, left in a store window overnight to confront passers-by with its asexual nudity. De Sade is a fiction composed by a fiction. Look for me in a late-night window, an after-hours bar, a white shuttered apartment above the Pont D'Orléans overlooking a leaf-green Seine, the eddies sequinned by twinkling patterns shaken out of the poplars. I am whatever you make of me. I was the non-person who faced courts, the hollow body whom they indicted and scarified as inhuman. The gravity of the sentence fell on a mummy. I was somewhere else and someone else. In my imagination I was in Amsterdam, standing on an eyebrow bridge watching the river trade, quizzing the red-light district, a man without a name or identity to the crowds, just anyone, a blank space concerned with its inner thoughts.

And is there an end to it, what I have done and what I will do? My eyes have stayed open on the world like someone condemned never to sleep. And in the long night, by which I mean one that takes in decades, centuries, I have seen the interior of life, the temporal infrastructure in relation to changes in the stars. I have watched the impetus in man to auto-destruct expand from iron to nuclear fission. The executioner going to work through the dawn streets, hands bunched into his raincoat, his eyes reading the pavement in their downward stare, has been replaced by the scientist, his car slipping through traffic, his mind insulated by music from a cassette, his identity number ready for security. What I achieved through orgasm is so much in advance of the splitting of the atom.

'I made myself agreeable to fifteen men; I was fucked ninety times in twenty-four hours, both in front and behind.' I remember that extract. Today I would quadruple it. There are de Sade imitators. They remind me of pink and green sugared mice under glass in a pâtisserie.

Philippe. Often I consider calling him. Did he return to designing ostentatious clothes for exhibitionists, or did the experience of La Coste drive him underground, into the reclusion of a monastery, an ashram, a cult who meditate on the virtues of inner space, to vegans, yogis, takers of hallucinogens? I have the number of his shop, his apartment, but he is for ever associated with a time and a place. I have to move on. There will always be others. There will always be me, a mind unable to break down the past or to forget. Sometimes I have the driver park up at the edge of a field, miles from anywhere. In these anonymous places I lose all notion of the century in which I live. Scarlet poppies, blue cornflowers blow at the edge of a field: this could be anywhere. A black cloud saunters slowly into a white; the two build to a piebald conglomerate on the horizon. I release a champagne cork and lie back and wait for the rain. It will come, drumming on the car roof, inducing a state of trance in which I review the past, the blinding momentum of the future.

When we move off, the car hardly audible on the wet, blue road, I encounter names from my past, characters who were pivotal in contributing to my ascesis of indulgence. Let me recall some of them, figures from my inexhaustible inventory of perversions. Noirceuil, Saint-Fond, Clairwil, Brisa-Testa, the Princess Borghese, Queen Charlotte, Duclos, Pope Pius VI. They were real and imaginary; they are constellations in the fetishistic imagination. I am always someone escaping to a point in timelessness. After the last filling-station with its attendant in orange overalls, the last boarded-up white bungalow strung out on a promontory at the end of the world, there exists a parallel world into which I escape. The crushed, peeling beer cans form a metallic surf, a glitter-line before the big drop into the sea. Cars park there at night, the curious stray there by day. To me it's not a stopping point from which to confront the broad sweep of a lighthouse, it's a cross-over place, a bridge.

In a month it will be autumn again, a drift of red leaves will cover the world. I've decided to telephone Philippe when the rains set in. If necessary we will take the car to Paris and park outside his home, his business. He will know it's me by the car, the tinted glass of a fractionally rolled-down window. And it will be raining. He will run out to the car, naked under a thigh-length leather coat, and our story will begin all over again.

Six

There was this man. He wanted me to paint a series of pictures magnifying the brutal death of the Princess de Lamballe, the assumed lesbian lover of Marie-Antoinette, who was decapitated by the mob and dragged headless through the streets of Paris. I will spare you the knowledge of her dismemberment. And when he came to my studio for the first time, he had to conceal his excitement over the details of her death, writing them down in order to control the spasmodic twitching in his face and hands. The first time he arrived here, when he came up to my attic flooded by an aquatic violet light, he looked old, chased out of his grey skin, adipose, cumbersome, his mind shifting focus on a kaleidoscopic fragmentation of thought. He was ursine. He waded rather than walked; he seemed unsure of the fluency of space around him, as though he had spent his lifetime in measuring out the dimensions of a cell. He appeared surprised by the elasticity of his movements. His sight was bad; he betrayed the caution of a blindfolded person who walks with his hands stretched out in front of his body, anticipating imaginary obstacles. A wall, a lamp-post, a person. The edge of a vertical drop to nowhere.

This man had suffered deeply; he nursed internal and external scars. Periodically he conducted a dialogue with himself interspersed with obscenities.

I requested he sit down, but despite his audible lack of breath he insisted on moving tentatively around my floor space. He was searching for something that couldn't be found, some loose connection which had come unwired in his head.

When he returned to the studio three weeks later he was unrecognizable, yet I knew him instantly by his blue eyes, which appeared to be coloured with drops fallen from the sky, by his small feminine mouth, and by the intensity of nervous energy transmitted by his features. He was slim, the ballast cut from him as though with a sculptor's knife, his manner fluent, worldly, cushioned by wealth, but secretive, as if he were inwardly searching for some means of escape from the labyrinth. I could almost hear him think. I imagined his head suddenly turned transparent and the coloured images generated by his mind showing through: the disconnected, transient flashes of so many incomplete narratives. Was he reviewing the past or the future, or had the two formed a textural consistency, a wash in which figurative characters stood out, pointing the one way of thought which is to disappear?

He was dressed in an expensive grey suit. Saint Laurent or Balmain. His shirt was tangerine, his tie a livid sunset-orange. He carried his apparent wealth with ease, but he looked like someone who never adopts a place of rest, living in hotels, a chain of apartments opened up only for transient visits: Paris, Nice, London, Madrid, New York. Such men are solitary; they are engaged in a voyage of inner discovery, a sort of oneiric journey which acquires the momentum of the somnambulist.

This time he introduced himself simply as de Sade. He formally detached a black velvet glove and extended his right hand. My own hands were confettied with paint blobs. I was wearing patched denim jeans and a white T-shirt on which Madonna's face was printed, her scarlet pouting lips accentuating her Monroe look-alike image.

I knew what the man wanted, and it was unfinished. His written instructions demanded a perversity of detail I felt unwilling to execute. His requirements read like extracts from a torture manual. It was as if he remembered the brutal decapitation of the Princess de Lamballe and wanted to get back there mentally. In her dismemberment he was clearly seeking some form of self-realization. If one perception leads directly to another, de Sade was trying to reactivate a dormant memory cell with the hope that the attendant implosion would connect with a hidden narrative.

All I had attempted was a series of scarlet brush-strokes denoting the violence, a textural abstraction superimposed on a square head with the notion of an extravagant black hat plume somehow connected with a flat cranium. But the red had taken off, it had become an autonomously directed vermilion, a seething clash of poppies, or blood escaping in a jet from a severed artery.

De Sade had an infallible sense of preconception. Instead of having me explain my partial and tentative beginnings, the sketches in which I was still only peripherally approaching his requirements, he took out a grey snakeskin wallet made inelegant by the wad of paper money wedged between its flaps. He asked me for the use of my brushes, took out quantities of notes and proceeded to paint them in bright primary colours. Scarlet, yellow, blue. He did this with a concentration, an overstated avidity as though he was showing me the experimental technique he had evolved over years of secret labour. He covered the table and its surrounding area of wooden floor with his painted money. And then he stopped and fixed me with his blue eyes.

'This is a reverse process,' he said. 'I paint money and you paint in order to earn money.'

He was silent. His thoughts had gone off at a tangent. A light rain spotted the skylight. The drops stayed there like little glass insects which had parachuted down out of a foreboding mauve sky. His coldness was brutal, imposing, reverberating through the studio. The rain quickened its staccato beat. And at the same time a perianth of light was opening in the cloud-ceiling. It washed across us as if we had been transposed dramatically from a dark room into sunshine.

De Sade opened a grey leather valise. He took out a writing pad and opened it, checked it momentarily and then handed it to me. It was what I had anticipated. It was a passage copied from his *120 Days of Sodom*. His handwriting was tiny. He asked me to read out what he had written.

'"Another individual, with similar tastes," Duclos went on, "took me to the Tuileries a few months later. He wanted me to proposition men and have them six inches from his face while he hid under a pile of deck-chairs; and after I had fucked seven or eight casual passers-by, he settled himself on a bench by one of the busiest paths, lifted my skirt from behind, and displayed my ass to whoever was passing. He then ordered me to blow him within view of half of Paris, something which despite the lateness of the hour, created such a scandal that by the time he had achieved his pleasure, we were surrounded by a group of ten spectators, and were forced to make off through the bushes to avoid the park police."'

'That's the most anaemic of my vignettes,' Sade commented. 'It's an aperitif to the pathologized lyricism by which I expressed every form of sexual aberration. And do you realize that I carry the potential within me, not only of committing atrocities, but of devising crimes the like of which this world has never known? Sadism disarms the power of nuclear threat. What are the possibilities inherent in the heat-flash compared to the way in which I would have things end?'

His inflexionless voice was the result of long inner study. For the first time in my life I realized how a person could contain within him a perfected blueprint to subvert the cycle of planets. Inner space represented for him a form of sexual fission. But I went along with him, I was compelled to entertain the nature of his thought, secretly fascinated by his constrained mannerisms, which were in violent contrast to the schema of his ideas.

He kept a thin, red-ended brush between the forefinger and index finger of his right hand, as though he was toying with a cigarette. The utensil afforded him a balance by which to measure his speech.

'You probably consider Bacon's anamorphs disturbing,' he continued. 'Muscular raw-meat torsos, mouths open, contorted, expressing the epiphanic agony of being. To me, they are too tame to arouse interest. If Bacon has gone further than

93

anyone in inventing a new anatomy to express a genocidal century, then I went still further, and continue to do so. Munch, Soutine, Modigliani, Picasso, Miró, Bacon. Look at the heads they paint. They present the facial change not in terms of how we look but of how we feel. They depict the ravaged schizoid doubles who occupy the space inside our heads. We all inhabit a wounded interior. I wanted to externalize mine and live out the reality rather than the fiction of its existence. When you show someone something which they think to be ugly, they have eventually to find beauty in it. And if you keep on repeating the experiment you may reverse the pattern by which they establish aesthetic values.

'I had to learn that. But that's not your concern. Let us say that I was shut away from the world. And this was the greatest freedom I could have been offered. They thought I was a captive monster walled up behind granite and steel, but I was the inhabitant of a place to which no one else has ever been. I was its solitary occupant. Sometimes I would hear the distraught shrieks of a man to whom the guards gave my name. His belligerence, his obscenity, his despair irritated me. I wanted to be left in peace at the centre of my kingdom, where no one could break in. And I was busy. I had to build my refuge out of the imagination. There wasn't anyone to help. Writing is like constructing a mental pyramid, only it deconstructs while one is building it. Paintings can be cleaned, restored, but words never can. Dead books are like scrapped cars; you could fill a continent with disposable literature, but you wouldn't find de Sade's works in that wasteland. Open the pages and the words sit on you like vultures. They eviscerate, strangle, lacerate, hysterectomize, decapitate. My words are restless. They live like torturers in search of victims. They want to re-enact my imaginings over and over again, to be slowed down, speeded up, rearranged, regrouped. I want to apply Burroughs's technique to my long novels. Imagine it, de Sade cut-ups continuing to be published throughout the twenty-first century. Endless permutations on a single theme. Sodomy. And the author invisible, anonymous, working on the edge of the world.'

He paused and looked up at the skylight. The colours were

changing. The clouds looked like a Sam Francis hash of colour. Like a palette thrown at an off-white wall and sticking there. Contusions, stellar reverberations of colour, spiral-arabesques standing out in violet, violent turquoises, sanded pinks. I wanted to paint that composition, call it *De Sade Improvisation No. 134*, but he continued, resuming his monologue as one might take up a drink after a rhythmic delay in conversation.

'What is new? Nothing. To the gourmet, a fillet of human flesh is the equivalent of chicken. His digestive juices assimilate both. And for the coprophiliac it's no different. Taste accommodates thought. The repulsive, the taboo, are simply those things which we are instructed to repel rather than attract. Your reluctance to paint the variations of a theme which I have commissioned conforms to that rudimentary principle. You imagine you'll go mad if you let go of a certain way of seeing, of experiencing life. You have to turn yourself inside out in order to create. You have to go one stage further than standing things on their head; you have to be prepared to up-end that process and the one that follows and so on. After you've stopped recognizing immediate perceptions you begin to create.'

When he paused again, I could feel the heat in the room transmitted by his thought, generated by his blood. And it wasn't that I wished him gone, out of the studio and back to whatever hermetic life he pursued travelling from place to place, but that I wanted to hear more. I was magnetized. He could have strangled me and I would have offered no resistance. I couldn't look directly into his face or eyes to find the source of this attraction. I felt submissive, concessionary, as though somehow my life and aspirations were unrealized, frustrated. I sensed the incipient stirrings of adventure. This man could lead me on a journey to the centre of the universe. He might take a detour from the main road, that metal artery thugged by container lorries, and at a short distance show me La Coste. The gates and house would be glossed by dark ivy; a naked woman would be sitting reading by a fountain, her right foot toying with a discarded shoe. She wouldn't even look up to see us pass.

'And let me instruct you', he resumed, in a manner that announced a monologue, 'in those things that we call the shadow. The dark side of life, the underworld, the backside of human nature. It's where exploration begins, Stephen. You can choose to join me there and return enriched in experience for your art, or you can remain within the sensory precinct in which you feel you are comfortable.

'You were to me a name. Stephen Vaughan. When I came across your work in that small but prestigious exhibition, I decided to go in search of you. I wanted to implant something foreign in your work, an impulse which would have it digress from inculcated aesthetics. And I collect; my position in life allows for that. Should I decide I want a Picabia, a Man Ray, an Yves Tanguy, a Braque, Klein or Dufy, a de Kooning or Kitaj, I can have whatever painting most readily accommodates my mood at the time. There are days on which my rebellious nature would rather have a Warhol or Trevor Winkfield than a Bonnard or Vuillard. I pursue nothing but my instincts.

'But my real concern is with erotica. And I am still searching for an artist who will shock me in the way that my writings terrorize conventional taste. I am looking for the visual representation of my scatology, someone able to evoke the pathological myth inherent in coprophilia, in sodomy and those rites which end in the most extreme forms of torture. That's the shadow side of me. You can believe it or not.

'There's a version of my life which has me die in the asylum of Charenton. I'm portrayed as obese, blind, asthmatic, someone whose physical deterioration matches their senility. But I'm credited with having devised games for the inmates, with having written plays which were performed by a psychotic cast. Biographers concede that much at the end. A redemptive quality to counteract putrefaction. Can you see me lumbering about with props, officiating over dress rehearsals, screaming raucously on an unlit stage? The writing is a different thing. Most of my plays were lost. Today I store what I write in a computer memory. You see, I had always to be someone and never no one. And I will always be that.'

I let him reconnect with his theme. He was ranging inwards, looking for points of reference in his mental flux, signposts which would stand up and demand attention. He had seen so much, gone so deep, journeyed to the bottom of the night and returned with what? A rat cupped in his hands? A gold swastika? A blue meteorite fallen from the blue sky? I found myself uncapping a bottle of Black Bush whiskey and pouring copious slugs into two tumblers. At first he hardly noticed his, but when he did, he drained it without so much as observing the level in the glass.

'I'm the progenitor of an occult sexual geometry,' he resumed. 'There's a privacy afforded everyone, a dimension on which a man operates independent of society. It's the one thing for which he's answerable to himself. It's like the dark space inside a cupboard. If it walked out by itself as a black block of brooding air, it would terrify. There's no answer to the lining of things. They live on the other side of sensory perception. In the sexual act you have to imagine what you feel. You're somewhere and nowhere. I wanted to externalize that inner conundrum, expose everything to the eye. And that's what people couldn't take: the visualization of erotic experiment. Seeing has never been a part of sex. The mathematics of the experiment are complex. Having read *The 120 Days of Sodom*, you'll remember the hundred and fifty Complex Passions. It would take a painting of the scope of Picasso's *Guernica* to interpret my imaginings. Twenty-seven might offer a theme for depiction: "He kisses the asshole of one girl while a second does the same to him and a third girl works at his prick. They then exchange tasks, so that by the end, each of the three has her ass kissed, each works at his prick, each frigs his ass." Simple, economical, but defiantly individual.'

The more this man intimated his inner reserves, the closer I felt to him. There's a degree of outrage which strips one apart. He had succeeded in finding the give within me, the repressed motives which once unblocked looked to reciprocate his fetishistic propensities. I poured whiskey into my glass with no consideration for the unmeasured volume. I loaded him with a similar excess. I was eager to hear him continue.

'If you were to read history, biography, all of those aberrant and fallacious attempts to impose a fictional pattern on time, a chronology gained not from immediacy but from calculated retrospect, then you would read that I was fifty before I published a book. I needed the money. Imprisonment and the revolution had left me impoverished. I met a young publisher called Girouard, whose concerns like mine were with commercial gain. The revolution had placed a permanent red sunset over Paris. There was a livid scarlet in the sky, day and night. There were also processions of headless bodies observed walking through the streets at noon, or crossing a bridge at night. Blood was in the air, the scent of it, the density of its volume as it spilt from carotid arteries. A vermilion stain hung in the blue sky.

'I now had two books ready for press. The September Massacres had prepared the way for my work. The dismemberment of bodies, the savage collective hysteria which had instigated the guillotine, the brutal atrocities committed by the mob, found their mirror in writing which otherwise would have been banned. You may remember details. How a woman was deliberately infected with syphilis and the apertures of her body sewn up with a wax thread. My imagination suited the times. What I had imagined had in turn become a reality. Girouard's printing shop was in the rue du Bout du Monde. When I went there I had the suspicion I was being followed: footsteps would sound in my head, faces appear out of alleys. In one unlit passage a man was eating roast dog with the same avidity as if it were chicken. There was the question of *Aline and Valcour*. They had commenced printing; I could smell the printer's ink, but Girouard had royalist sympathies. The last time I saw him he was nervous, paper-faced, distracted, unable to concentrate, preoccupied with opening and closing the drawer of his desk, something he did with metronomic regularity, as though he needed to be assured that whatever he had destroyed was missing. But in his mind it was still there. A letter, a sheaf of papers, something which by its presence, real or imaginary, incriminated its owner.

'It was cold, a blue rime of ice sparkled on the cobbles. The air returned from one's lungs as effusive white tusks. When I entered the rue du Bout du Monde, the shop was boarded up.

I knew it without asking: Girouard had been guillotined on 8 January 1794. His head joined the other hirsute melons they stuck about the city on spikes as a grisly reminder to the masses that the individual must pay for his life in blood.

'When you live a life engaged in activities that are underground, subversive, obsessive, a century is no more than the blink of an eye. It disappears as a slight reddening of the cornea. I was in search of the ultimate sexual experience: I still am. You may find out that you are the person best suited to accommodate my experiments.'

I must have drowsed. The whiskey was still tight in my head, contracting my thinking space, squeezing the expansion of thought to the kernel-sized interior occupied by a nut. At first I thought it was I who was running at high speed, accelerating over flashback fields, landscapes in which goats stood out on crags, and then as the subdued hum of the engine fractionally changed its note, I realized that we were speeding in a car through open countryside. We were travelling fast, I could sense this despite the feeling of displacement in my head. We were burning somewhere, the light breaking up in planes over the car, my head cradled by the smell of leather upholstery.

I let myself surface slowly, and without looking I knew he would be there. He had retained the same alert composure, the look of a man who never knew the necessity of sleep, but had stayed awake for centuries, shooting up on amphetamines in the bathroom, adjusting his metabolism to the needs of the day, to the long vigil he maintained through the nights.

He was waiting for this moment. I had the impression that this pattern had repeated itself incessantly, the man and his displaced acolyte heading towards La Coste, the century irrelevant, the speech transferred to a tape-recorder, silently unwinding its magnetized loops from A to B. And was it I who had known this same road before, the feeling of inexorable coercion as gradually the man asserted his presence, and the fields jumped at the window and wouldn't stay?

Seeing me awake, he resumed his speech as though there had been no transition between places, no break in the monologue, only the most fractional of incursions on his thematic

99

concentration. I noticed the fluted glass in his hand. It was ticking with champagne. He was wearing cologne. Its name eluded me. The fragrance demanded I know, then backed off, antagonizing, coaxing, defying my olfactory interpretation. There was a goat on the road. We had to stop. The animal went off reproachfully, dazed by its confrontation with a machine. The two had no meeting place on this earth, unless it was in the shock of metal snapping bone.

He was talking again, this enigma called de Sade, this man who had shocked successive centuries with his advocacy of sexual torture. Perhaps he wanted me to paint for him at his home, discover within myself the perverse physical cosmos to which he was so attached.

'Another thirty minutes, and we'll be there,' he was saying. 'Once when I was arrested, I was informed that I would be shut up in a black room upstairs full of dead bodies. And I lived like that, inside a black honeycomb. I had my dead but they were within me. If I thought I could ever die, I would write my memoirs, the most shocking that ever existed. There's no way back from what I have done or what I continue to do. But while I'm alive the extent of my actions remains modified by what I choose to conceal. I can undo that through writing. I can expose secrets of a nature too intolerable for human nerves. There have always been Black Books. Occult sects, dictators, pornographers have given them concealment, cherished their disclosures as one might guard the scientific antidote to death. You may assume I have such a vaccine at La Coste, its cellular alchemy preventing the process of degeneration in me.'

I caught at bits of the flow, heard his syntax leak into my head. I didn't want to be back in my studio painting, forming incongruous connections between a red pumpkin, a silver pyramid and a black square. These images from my last work floated into view, together with the montage I had been preparing, working the assassinations of Kennedy, Martin Luther King and John Lennon into a vermilion skyline over New York. Already that work seemed to belong to another time, another place, a different lifetime. Deep within me was the conviction that I had found my master, my sexual guru.

This information had been coded in my unconscious through oneiric experience, day-dreams in which I saw myself walking up the oak-shadowed drive of a château followed by a man who implanted his third eye into my back like a blue jewel. I used to imagine he had a sapphire in the eye of his penis.

'You won't lack anything where we are going,' he resumed. 'What would you do if you knew that my château contained the serum which imparts deathlessness? Would you wish to be injected with minims of this fluid?'

He seemed suddenly exhausted. He averted his profile, turning his head in a semi-circle to look out at something which had accidentally caught his attention. A tree, a sign-post, a can jumping off the tyres? We were there.

A naked woman in purple leather thigh boots opened a gate so burdened with ivy that it was indistinguishable from the high hedge that ran along the lane. Its concealment was perfect. We drove slowly down a tree-bordered drive. If the car windows had been open we would have heard the surf of leaves turning over in the wind, seen the undersides of poplars and planes flashing silver. I wasn't allowed a glimpse of the gothic façade. The car was driven down to a garage in the subterranean depths of the house. Spotlights picked out a space which smelt of oil, of air that remained corked to ferment underground. A misanthropic reclusion.

We took an elevator which brought us out from behind the panelling of his bedroom. The walls were painted lavender. The furniture was black with gilt inlays. It felt cold and impersonal, as though rarely lived in, and even then it was to the exclusion of all human warmth. I had the feeling that we were so cut off from the world, so immured in a sound-proofed zone, that we had entered another dimension of being. No one could intrude on this man's meticulously devised interior. It was as if he had concealed the château inside a safe and buried that repository in the depths of the earth.

De Sade displayed his customary indifference, his accept-ance of any situation as conducive to his welfare. What he had was presence, the inimitable hauteur one perceives in a photo-graph by Man Ray, the depiction of a solarized Lee Miller or Nusch Eluard, the four raindropped eyes belonging to the

Marquise Cassati, the hoop-shaped bangles running up and down Nancy Cunard's arms while her eyes are somewhere else, chasing her thoughts into the black hole we call forgetting.

A butler came in and presented de Sade with a number of letters and a cassette in its plastic shell.

'I'll play you this later on,' he said, 'it will prove a revelation. I have an archive of tapes, many of which contain the sexual secrets of film-stars, celebrities, royalty, actresses, voyeurs, almost the entire social spectrum who have manifested an interest in one bizarre fetish or another. People have unaccountably peculiar tastes, but few have ever been a match for me. What has happened at La Coste over the centuries is the still-unwritten sexual history of the universe.

'And why I have brought you here is to have you photograph and paint the orgiastic excesses which will occur. You will have a studio with a dark-room attached. You may wish to be circumspect and view things through a two-way mirror. You have not been selected to participate in the sexual rites. Rather, you will observe, consider and create. I will have you stay two months in your time. You will be paid for this intermission in your life. For let me tell you, Stephen, that from now until you leave you are officially a missing person. Your friends will find no trace of you, hear no word from you. This château, La Coste, was reduced to ruins in 1790. To the public it remains a redoubtable reminder of the man they consider me to have been. On a parallel dimension I continue to exist here in comfort each autumn. Thereafter you may find me in one of twenty capitals. I go under many names and profess to heteroclite activities, but I am always Donatien-Alphonse-François de Sade. On that principle I have no equivocation. I cannot say your life will not be changed for having been here, it will, but in small, imperceptible ways to do with your memory cells, your apprehension of time.'

I was taken to my studio and adjoining bedroom by a girl dressed in a black silk top-hat and a leopard-spotted leotard. She balanced on eight-inch brittle scarlet heels. Already I was beginning to feel disconnected from my past, as though a shift had occurred in my perception of dreams and reality. I had the feeling that I belonged to neither state, and that what I was living through was something like autonomous trance. My physical responses appeared robotic; I was attuned to blurred, off-centre hypnagogic imagery. And by the time I had reached my room, which lay at the far end of a spiral corridor in which the subdued green lighting came from ceiling fixtures, my vision was beginning to buzz with intense colour. It was as though someone had internally manipulated a colour switch. Violets, emeralds, scarlets, saffrons, livid orange and purples imploded like hallucinatory supernovas. And it all happened without fear on my part. I was the spectator of riotously pyrotechnical film-frames: 3D images of fellatio, giant thighs hanging loose from dense lianas, an elephant walking on clouds as though they were snow underfoot. No amount of LSD or of its adulteration, Ecstasy, could have created this dynamic freak show. I remained hooked on a visual fantasia. I realized that the centre of the universe was luminous and not black. The further one travelled into deep space the more brightly coloured grew the expansive unknown. The microstructure of a cell was repeated in the galactic megatons of burning planets: corpuscle to star, the quantum leap was one of visualization.

I sat down on the bed and listened to my thoughts. They had developed a weird hum, the noise of bees interrogating the interior of snapdragons. Everything that happened to me within was magnified by the anacoustic depths of the château. My heartbeat sounded like a drum tattoo in the hills. A single movement made the room resound with disturbing frequency. Without reflecting on it, I realized that I had gone missing from the chronology imposed on time by my friends, by the normal routine of my working days. Anything could happen here. De Sade had told me of tigers he kept at the château, and whether he meant sexual partners dressed like big cats, or whether he was referring to the existence of real beasts, it was a detail which I couldn't dislodge from my mind. Everything was possible in this dimension: a circus, a theatre, a human zoo, a menagerie kept for perverse pleasures, the cloning of images into 3D reflections. La Coste vibrated with de Sade's fantasies, the ones about which he wrote, and those he acted out. And the two couldn't be separated here.

Dream and reality were interchangeable.

Once while I sat in my room under a lowering yellow autumn sky, I came across a love letter of his. It was dated 22 March 1779. I didn't know what year we were living in, so it had for me the immediacy of something he had just written:

New Year's Day has passed, and you did not visit me. I waited all through the long day. I had made myself attractive. I was wearing make-up and cologne, and not fur-trimmed boots but a pair of green silk stockings, red trousers, a yellow waistcoat with my long black tails, and a hat embroidered with silver. In a word, I looked my part as an aristocrat. A regiment of jam-jars was waiting, and I had even prepared a little concert: three drums, four kettledrums, eighteen trumpets and forty-two horns. . . .

Inadvertently the man had shown me another facet of his character. The self-indulgent romantic, forced out of dissimulation to depict himself as a lover, was the same man who had eaten rats captured in his cell at Charenton, and administered enemas to women queuing up outside his secret room, dressed as nuns.

And there were other times when I was permitted to telescope back into his past. If he visited me to go through a pile of photographs or a recently completed painting, I would anticipate his leaving behind some vestige to authenticate his identity. He was so distinctly modern, sitting in front of his IBM word-processor, scanning the blue screen, marking up the white lines of the interminably long novels he wrote, editing, revising, that I had to make a big leap in time to imagine him meticulously penning letters in his characteristically small hand.

And there were some things I read in snatches, for he would return without warning, his eyes fixed on the spot where he knew he had left a letter. He would pick it up without comment and disappear into one of the endless recesses which formed an underground labyrinth beneath the château.

I remember his sparkling wit. 'As long as I'm not rehabilitated, there won't be a cat whipped in the provinces without someone saying, "It's the Marquis de Sade."' And a passage to his wife: 'You ride beautifully in the wrong direction, know how to arouse, are strait in the gate and warm in the rectum, which means that we are ideally suited.'

I worked alone in my dark-room or in the studio. I had to print up magnified studies of male and female erogenous zones, complex geometric connections attained during the orgies that de Sade conducted in those rooms given over to his erotic expression, either as a participant or voyeur. I used a number of camera apertures that de Sade had constructed into a viewing room. I saw everything, but was never seen. I worked with an invisible presence, learning to detach myself from what I observed, thinking now and then that I recognized someone, despite the mask they wore as a precaution: a pop celebrity, a media personality, a member of the Government? All manner of people came here anonymously and left without ever knowing that their orgiastic excesses had been videoed by de Sade, and in addition committed to film by me. Of my work, de Sade would say, 'It's for the archives. Your contributions will be studied in future centuries. I have here at La Coste the blueprints for a new species who will evolve from certain rites of sex, certain anatomical readings which will go to establish new physiological forms.'

When I wasn't working I sat and listened. I was waiting for someone to help set me free. When and how that would come about became a constant preoccupation. I remember thinking it must have been like this for him all those centuries ago, his ear trained for the approach of leather boots, the jingle of heavy keys secured on a ring. Would it be today or in a hundred years that the door would open to admit light, the prison officer not even showing his face, keeping an averted profile, his boots smelling of polish, his uniform devoid of a single crease?

I worked with the sort of detachment I had once experienced in a breakdown at art college. During that illness, everything appeared unreal. Nothing I looked at in the physical world had any connection with me. Even if I went down on my hands and knees and touched the grass, the earth, the stone ensconced in its unmovable matrix, still nothing seemed possessed of tangible properties. And now, when I painted scenes that I had first photographed, enlarging on an aspect which I knew would gratify the obsessive fetish that de Sade had already made known to me, I might have been painting from a distance of several hundred yards. I couldn't establish contact or feel with my materials. It was as though my sense of time, inherited through the discipline of daily routine, resisted the assimilation into de Sade's timelessness.

And at night they would knock on my door, the girls and boys sent by de Sade to provoke me with their costumes, their uninhibited gestures. I would turn away a girl dressed in a spotted face-net, scarlet suspenders, black silk stockings and stilettos. Another would come to my room dressed in a fishnet body-stocking, still another in transparent panties to be followed by a boy in leather hot pants, one hand on his hip, a cigarette extending like a flower stem from his lipsticked pout. And I resisted them all. I had come to associate sex with the idea of unconsciousness, which in turn might leave me vulnerable to experimentation with the serum which de Sade had mentioned. What if he really did possess the solution he maintained would allow him to live for ever? Would I find myself in the next century, sitting beside this man in a chauffeur-driven car, almost the last survivors of a post-nuclear holocaust, our bodies forced together in love for lack of an alternative?

Night after night I turned them away: women, men, trans-vestites, transsexuals, whatever new contingent de Sade had brought to the château. And the faces rotated or disappeared. What happened to them after they left La Coste was an enigma which continued to puzzle me. Did they go about the world as strangers, people who could never again find a home, but were possessed of the illusion that they would return to de Sade's château? Only they could never reach it, and if they did, they were brought face to face with the shell, a ruin that had withstood the erosion of time but was nothing more than that. And perhaps unable to grasp this, they went away bitter, mad, tormented.

But if I refused their sexual favours, my loneliness at times led me to welcome their conversation. I used to speak to Mathilde, a girl who reappeared so persistently that I felt impelled to invite her into the studio. Dressed in a black sequinned bra and a red PVC micro-skirt, she seemed drugged, forced into the scheme of things, unwilling at first to talk, then by degrees growing less suspicious, relaxing enough to confide in me her name, her home town, her former occupation: a hairdresser. This girl with her face made up like a transvestite, her skin pigmented with gold scintillating powder, her skirt no more than a belt, her lipstick resembling a gloss-protected black bruise. She had been out walking one day, as one does in those restless moods when one goes out in search of some inexpressible impulse, the inner speed overtaking the outer, so that buildings fly by: a cinema, a supermarket, a department store, the graffiti scrawled across a fissured tenement, then the outskirts of town, the bad end that gives on to wasteland, cars cruising by with their windows rolled down in the chance of a pick-up. She wasn't conscious of going anywhere or of being anything but an endless stream of thoughts. She had disconnected from reality. And suddenly without warning, the car was there. Parked up ahead of her, a beetle-blue Mercedes, the glossy carapace taking the shine from a red sunset.

'The near door was open. He was hunched over on the far side, his face eaten up by dark glasses. The gesture had caught me out. I found myself stopping short, looking into the car's interior. I knew I had to get in, be driven away without so much as asking a question. It was my only course of action. I didn't wish to know where we were going or what was happening. Usually this sort of man wants a restaurant, a late-night spot, and then home to the outskirts of the city. An anonymous house, the money left under the pillow, his chauffeur waiting to deposit me somewhere at midday.

'There's no coming back with such men. No second time, unless you're special. There's always someone else, and that's what they'll let you know. People are so many blanks, a series of white zeros with dotted eyes.'

I let her sink into herself. People need that respite, the going back in as if there was a room inside the head in which one could sit down, arrange flowers, pull the blinds on the day outside.

'I had to come here,' I found myself saying to Mathilde. 'And clearly it was the same for you. It's his magnetism, and it must have happened with everyone. It's like being stretched across a black hole. I don't imagine one is ever the same person again.'

Mathilde bit a scarlet fingernail, the lacquer glossed to a blinding, Matisse vermilion. For a moment I had no idea if she was detained by her own absorption or if she was following my thought to its conclusion.

'There's lots of us, you know,' she said. 'You're privileged. You don't really see what's going on. They come and go, but sometimes there's a hundred people. He drugs us. He threatened me on arrival with an injection which would have me live for ever. Can you imagine that? Living here without even the prospect of death. And now I don't know how long I've been his captive. It might have been three days ago or three years that I set out for that walk. Thirty years, three hundred years, it hardly matters. And when he puts you back outside, I'm told, you don't even know who you are.'

Mathilde, who had been sent here ostensibly for my distraction, had relaxed sufficiently to impart knowledge both about herself and the place.

'Who is this man?' I asked. 'He claims to be the Marquis de Sade, someone who has overcome the biological process of death. Someone who perpetuates himself through the centuries.'

Mathilde didn't answer. She had drifted away. She was adjusting a black lace stocking top to a red suspender strap. She completed the act with the obsessive concentration of someone who half expects to uncover a revelation by the completion of a fetish. She sat on the bed, both legs arched up to pronounce the curve of her stocking seams, checked her lipstick in a compact, then went out of the door as though we'd never met.

I followed her walk the length of the corridor. She might have been heading for the other side of the world from the isolation that came back to me, the oppressive feeling that I was working in a lighted cabin at the bottom of the sea. How long would this go on? And yet I had little desire to return to my former ways. What I felt was a sense of irreparable disconnection from the past and present. Would I end up marrying this man in a weird ceremony conducted in his theatre?

I looked at the series of sketches I had done for a painting which was to be called *Dark-Room 3*. There were no faces, only bottoms. This was at de Sade's dictate; he could only relate to the blank side of a person. I would normally have felt distaste for the subject matter, lacking all understanding as I did of such sexual preferences, but I had begun to execute my work almost autonomously. It might have been someone else's photography and painting that I contemplated, that of a stranger whom I could consider without emotional involvement, an objective assessment of something I viewed in terms of technique.

I had become used to de Sade entering my room without warning. If I was asleep, I would be woken by his quiet voice taking up its accustomed monologue. And it was always as though there had been no break in our previous conversation. I had begun to think that his mind comprised a magnetized tape, a cassette he was able intrinsically to stop at a certain point and restart in a manner appropriate to his new train of thought. A to B and back again, in an unbroken cycle, rather like his life.

When he knocked at the door it was with the authority of someone who was already on the other side. He was dressed in one of his favourite grey silk suits, an orange shirt and black tie snowed with orange polka dots. His place in life was always slightly off-centre, as though his confidence allowed him to drift wide of immediate issues. He was already the future by way of his detachment from the present.

'You have still to shock me,' he said, in his inflexionless tone. 'I need the sort of kicks you are too inhibited to express. When you go back to the world one of these nights it will be as one who has not escaped death. You'll be someone still searching for clues to the insoluble enigma of life, someone still inflicted with the phylogenetic memory of death, the degeneracy of the cells. You won't have advanced. You will remember this time as an interlude in life. The memory of it will seem like a string of images encountered in a dream. Perhaps that is how it will come back to you, as something jerky, indeterminate, a series of incidents which may or may not have happened. And then you'll come in search of me. You'll spend years on the road looking for La Coste, driving round and round in convoluted circles. Your money and life will be exhausted in the search for an illusion. And not content with that, you'll continue your search in other capitals, enquiring if I exist, describing me to total strangers, bribing janitors and security men to let you into apartment blocks where I have never lived. And in the end you will find yourself a vagrant, someone who steals or busks to earn a subsistence.'

I listened to his voice, certain he was establishing a fiction, a way of life to which I would never subscribe. The silence after he had stopped speaking was so oppressive, so loud in its articulation of nothing that its pressure seemed to be blowing me back in slow-motion, as though I was watching a film with the sound turned off. There was momentarily no future: nowhere to go because everywhere was occupied. If I tried to escape I would be lost in the endless maze of tunnels; if I was dismissed from La Coste I might find myself in a century of which I had no knowledge. And I believed this. I had allowed the idea to occupy me. In my mind I could see myself stepping out into a universe post World War IV or V. The sun was a dusty red, there were no cars on the road, villages and towns stood in ruins, blasted by reverberations after the heat-flash. No birds, no trees, no recognizable landscape. Just cities in dust. A whole line of skeletons flaked by ash, still sitting in red and green deck-chairs on a beach. On the outskirts of a dead city, the fifty thousand who had attended a rock concert that afternoon were one collective scar, a geometry of the living twisted into the agonized extremities of catastrophe. And in one way I was already experiencing it. I had overtaken the present and was participating in what I knew to be the future.

It was Mathilde who came for me the following night. Or

110

was it day? Time didn't exist within de Sade's château. Pivoting on purple leather heels, constricted by a black skirt into which she must have been sewn, she arrived without warning or explanation. I knew I had to follow. My time here had been unprofitable to de Sade. I was going back to whatever existed outside his province. I followed Mathilde down corridors into lifts and the process was endlessly repeated. I was beginning to think that there was no way out, that at some point she would admit defeat and deposit me in a similar room with an identical studio attached to it, a clock without hands looking me full in the face like a newly risen moon.

We explored *impasse* after *impasse*, doubled on ourselves, went up vertically, always under the same muted light, always within the same soundproofed walls. The experience was like that of having lived and died on a unilateral plane. There wasn't anything or anyone to return to, my memory existed only for the duration of my stay at La Coste. I was the product of de Sade's mind, a satellite generated by his fantasies. The impersonal surroundings, the impression of a labyrinth reminded me of an airport terminal.

And then quite suddenly a door opened out into the light. I turned round to speak to Mathilde but she was gone. I found myself in the middle of a field. The light hurt my eyes. My breathing was rapid. My first instinct was to run back and take shelter in the building I had left. But it was no longer there. I could hear a car on the road in the distance, and after a long pause another. I headed that way. I figured someone would be driving in the direction of life, towards a capital. That way I might begin to reacquaint myself with my past, the meaning of my being here. The sky really was blue. A few clouds seemed too immobilized to be going anywhere.

Seven

We begin again. Not once upon a time, but now, in the immediacy of the moment. I am someone and no one, a face screened out by black mirror glasses behind the bullet-proof windows of my limousine. How did I come to get here, to be always on the road, heading through towns which are sleeping, Amsterdam, Cologne, Stuttgart, a pink light showing through the blue-black dawn? We never stop. This engine like my heart goes on beating for ever.

I am who? At the risk of repeating myself: Donatien-Alphonse-François de Sade.

My father called me to Paris that winter and I hurried to him: his health was failing, and he wished to see me settled before he died; this project and the pleasures of the town diverted me . . . I spent two years in pursuit of my obsessions.

You can read this as autobiography in the same way as the fact that at the age of four I went to stay with my grandmother at Avignon. Or that at ten I attended the college of Louis-le-Grand as a day boy. There I was taught music, dancing, fencing. I also spent a lot of time looking at paintings in the Louvre: Titian, Tintoretto, Veronese, their names have withstood erosion. Today I might prefer an Yves Klein, a

Hockney, a Lichtenstein. My moods vary in accordance with what I remember of the past, the continuous present. The road unwinds before me: a nuclear-power plant here, over there the aircraft-hangar dimensions of a silo, poppies trailing a blaze of red silk by a grizzled cornfield. The future is like an ongoing movie – I need to see the faces, the changes, the cataclysmic catastrophes. This girl, dressed in a leather cap and a silver zipper-suit, blows cigarette smoke into her female lover's mouth. When they kiss it's like the joining of two scarlet ovals. I am the eye watching, the one who misses no sexual act. And aren't we moving into the polysexual future I predicted in *The 120 Days of Sodom*, the world of multiple erotic permutations at least accorded a degree of the tolerance that I instigated in my writings? When the car punches a beer can off the crown of the road I'm reminded of the transience of things.

At a time when I thought myself perishable, constrained by temporal limits, conscious of the degeneration of my organism, aware of my separation by being confined to a cell, I attempted to argue for posthumous recognition, as though that could mean anything in a world in which millions have not only dug their own graves, but also considered the past in the way one scoops up sand on the dunes at Arcachon and allows its sparkling granules to sift through one's fingers. I wanted the fame I have outlived by going on to create a life and a body of work which is still unknown. It was I who wrote:

I should like to find a crime with perpetual repercussions, one which would resonate after my death, so that there would not be a single instant of my future in which I would not be generating disorder, a subversion the equivalent of revolution, a perversion by which my name would live for ever.

Today, I would rewrite my intentions:

Look for me at the end of the world. After the heat-flash, the planet's extinction. My car will be parked on the edge of a cliff. I shall be looking out at the radioactive sunset, a man in a blue sequinned dress sitting on my knee.

Is this statement any more reliable than its predecessor? Aren't we all fictional embodiments trying to prove our claim to reality? Tonight I may find myself in the Paris Ritz or parked up beside a field. The two lovers in a nearby car are so preoccupied they do not notice me. They have a window open for the cool night air. The woman's voice tinkles like piano keys across the divide. She is being tickled the way a pianist touches the ivories.

I inhale the fragrant air. It smells of camomile and feverfew. The night is the book in which we write in dragon's blood. If a man came running across this field, shouting of catastrophe, his face covered by a white mask through which blood escaped, would I be surprised? And of what war would he be the messenger? One of the thousands I have lived through, or the televised nuclear offensive, the big impact watched by viewers unaware that they are witnessing their own deaths and the extinction of the planet? A fiction by Ballard realized as a historic event.

My world and yours. If I took it to extremes I might say our world, only that there is no reciprocal truth in that notion. I am one of the unassimilated. If the process began as a child when my seething temper cut into the young Prince Louis-Joseph, rocking him bone by bone from his physical axis, then my tangential hold on life will end in some eschatological catastrophe. Sometimes I contemplate the act of final madness, the man who will blow up the planet and remain immune to the consequences. And after that, where is there to go, what is there to do? Will the car still driven by the same chauffeur pick its way through the post-nuclear ruins? Will I find somewhere on the road a news kiosk which has escaped the flash, the bare-bottomed girls depicted in *Playboy*, *Mayfair*, *Penthouse* still positioned to attract the rush-hour crowd? Or somewhere in the concrete ziggurat of suburbia, a line of shop mannequins standing to the side of the road, marking the site where a store once stood?

Whenever we stop thinking, imagining a continuity, the abyss intrudes. The film-frames demonstrate the black jumps in the visual sequence. A police car, its lights tucked low, just flickered past on the road behind us. And if they'd stopped? I am the impeccable *haute couture* sophisticate, the man whose apparent elegance and sobriety is invincible. Would the condescending brute in the midnight-blue uniform know that he was confronting a passenger who had been held up on the roads of Savoy in the eighteenth century? And in the carriage, slewing from one mud rut to another, the horses whipped to a froth, the impression of standing still on a moving road was magnified until it became intolerable and I screamed, SCREAMED to shake myself out ui the apparent inertia of mobility. If we hadn't cleared the frontier they would have taken me back to France in chains. I would have been paraded through the streets of Paris like a circus bear, a man brought low by his fixation with the anal sphincter. The scapegoat, the pariah asked to suffer for the hypocrisy of the times. Aren't politicians the oleaginous parasites on a financial sore, a wound they stake out as their own, a whole cabinet siphoning blood through cocktail straws?

The older I get, the more I read about myself. 'De Sade's insanity lay more in his refusal to go mad, when everyone and everything condemned him to go mad.' But at that time I was stone, a petroglyph inscribed on the walls of the Bastille, Vincennes, Charenton. Someone whose blood had coagulated. When I worked myself to a white heat I had the Bastille blow with me. My orgasm lifted Paris into the sky.

We will move on tonight. I have my apartments, La Coste, but I have no stopping point. The summer still burns; a glowering heat scorches the noon and at night there's no air. I have to wait for autumn, the cyclic return of my sexual frenzy. In an hour it will thunder. I can hear the first reverberations. It starts as a pebble dislodged from a summit into a gorge, and builds to a freak wave slamming into a cove. At La Coste the autumn lightning storms are a perfect accompaniment to our nocturnal orgies.

And autumn is the time of mushrooms, fungi, with their phallic connotations. Remember my creation, the giant

Minski. And my description of his penis: 'a sausage, about eighteen inches long and sixteen inches round, topped with a scarlet mushroom as wide as the crown of a hat'. And these are not teratological fantasies. They are the perceptions of senses so magnified that a leaf vibrates with the intensity of a star, an ant grows to the proportions of a stampeding elephant, a follicle to the width of a strangulating liana. The increase in adrenalin causes everything to implode. It's like that in sex. One's fantasies grow protean; they threaten to overtake one's body space, grow so huge we are forced out and into another dimension. The Japanese girl with her legs open scissor-kicks clean through one on a journey to Mars.

If I wēnt right back to beginnings, found myself in a state of pre-natal apprehension, anticipating a future that was still unrealized, and not as yet attuned to its karma, then I might know myself as someone starting out on a journey that has no end. D.A.F. de Sade. A person free of the name that attaches to me, the inexorable infamy that must always accompany me.

At La Coste I have a video archive which collates a reconstructed past with the present. I have spent my time reenacting the sexual encounters described in *Justine*, *Juliette* and *The 120 Days of Sodom*, translating them from the verbal into the visual, from the imagined into the erotically enacted. And there's a discrepancy in this; language like sex undergoes a process of constant updating. Anatomy too has changed; the lubricious wads of flesh apparent even in my minors have been replaced by a leaner species, a race aware of aerobics, gym work-outs with weights, saunas, jacuzzis, cosmetic surgery. What I have on film is an approximate retrieval of my diverse consummations. Only the direction never falters. I enter by the back way. Make of that what you like. Only remember what I wrote of the Bishop in *The 120 Days of Sodom*, that he 'never committed a crime without immediately conceiving a second'.

Reading about oneself is like being introduced to a stranger. But I keep an eye open for new appraisals. After Lély, Foucault, Bataille, de Beauvoir, Klossowski, I find in Annie Le Brun's *Soudain un bloc d'abîme, Sade* a sympathy seldom seen in her critical predecessors. Here is a theoretical book to delight me, one in which the dialectic is sensitized by the lyricism of a poet. I could telephone and arrange an appointment, but she wouldn't believe it was me. Her work rests on the assumption that I am dead, that my extant corpus may include recently discovered works from the past, but not additions from the future. De Sade has grown to be a Swiss lake, the water measurable in terms of width and depth; and blue, as though the sky had kept on falling into an oval hole.

Tonight I want the privacy of a hotel suite. There is so much I have to sift through, mentally and physically. Lying on a bed, my feet tucked into white socks and black ballet shoes, a style I adopt both for comfort and elegance, I have the world at my disposal through a telephone.

The night is a sky ceiling constellated by memory. A glass ticks in my hand; the hotel is insulated by dark-green carpets. The silent lift hardly registers in its ascent from floor to floor. And if time played a trick, captured as in a photograph the faces stepping out at a particular moment in history, *circa* 1930, wouldn't I expect the low knock at my door to usher in Adolf Hitler, Antonin Artaud, Aleister Crowley and, three decades later, Mick Jagger, R.D. Laing and a child who answers to no name as he bounces a silver ball on the carpet and exposes the star tattoo on his left shoulder. He is one of the Western revolutionaries sworn to avenge himself on those who have disinherited the occult as the primary motivation of world governments. And there's a fourth, who arrives late. It is William Burroughs, hat slouched over his vulturine face, silk tie-knot straggling loose from a Brooks Brothers button-down-collar shirt, his features etiolated to chicken ribs by heroin. He's a walking cobweb with a Southern drawl. And a fifth? It might be Jean Genet, his grizzled convict's head bowed, his small stature clamped into bruised leather and denim, his eyes speaking of autumn, loss, the migration of years known from the unchanging constriction of a cell.

When I stay in a hotel, I book an entire floor. That way I'm left to myself. A bleep connects me to my chauffeur, another to a doctor, and so on. And what of *Juliette*, that novel which even as late as 10 January 1957 was declared by the Commission du Livre 'an outrage to public morals'? I take up a copy of a new translation of the book and think how poorly it compares to the version I have on disc.

> I'll give her an occasional slap on the face while I
> bugger dear little Eglée; and two of the boys will take
> turns sounding my bum, while I'll pluck hairs first from
> Henriette's cunt, and then Lolotte's, all the time
> watching Lindane and Juliette getting it, one in the cunt,
> the other in the asshole, from two coolly detached youths.

No one has ever read my books, at least not from beginning to end. Readers dip in at random to appease a particular fetish, or recoil from the scatological nature of the contents. But if one is to complete the journey, going by way of the variants and permutations of the text, one will arrive at a new understanding of the universe, purged by the reconciliation of one's inhibitions with natural desire. Amongst modern novels I find a similar awareness in Ballard's *Crash*, a book which marries eroticism to the lesions created by road deaths, the head-on collision of two cars on the perimeter roads leading to Heathrow. Getting high on abrasions, the extreme positions of crash victims, still wrapped around their metal interiors or ejected on to a brutal concrete surface. I read, make no mistake about that. Living anonymously, out of time and place and historic association, affords me freedom. But I demand engagement, dynamism, lines that buzz through my veins like adrenalin. Complacency is the inveterate enemy of creation. Writing is like walking over shards of glass with bare feet: the blood serves as a reminder of the pain encountered.

In 1799, the *Journal de Paris* and the press in general reported that I was dead. It was an attempt on the part of the media to be rid of me. If the author of *The New Justine* and *Juliette* was deceased, then the scandal surrounding the books I had already disowned in the interests of safety would be the more easily extinguished. The same year found me destitute, evicted from the apartment at Saint-Ouen, near Paris, which had proved a temporary refuge. Was it fear induced the schizoid split in my personality, or did I dissociate myself from my work to a degree whereby I could attribute its origins to a stranger? I had attempted to find employment as the curator of a library or museum in order to support Marie-Constance, with whom I was living. And in reality we were close to vagrancy, my silk shirt exchanged for holed linen, my gloves stained from the street, and finally not gloves at all, but damaged fingers, hands which were rashed blue and purple. And after weeks and months they became objects I could not contemplate. The white gloves I wear today are a reminder never to take for granted those most sensitive of all instruments. They had covered thousands of miles across paper, they were the balancing and communicating points of my mind. The right hand had worked for me through exhaustion and a cold so extreme in the Bastille that my wrist wore a bangle of blue ice.

Before the New Year of 1800, I had been picked up in the street, dying of starvation. Anything would have been palatable. The dead body of a vagrant, a sewer rat, the gristle from a horse binned at the meat market. Instead I became obsessed with the fantasy of eating myself. There was nothing else left. In the way that people today sell their blood in order to live, so I envisaged reducing myself, letting pieces go by a process of auto-cannibalism. And my debts: they had escalated to pyramidal proportions. I owed Renée Pélagie a hundred and sixty thousand livres in consequence of our separation. If I had an address to own to, it was the back of a barn in Versailles. Writing was made hard by the invasion of that private space I had known in my long years of confinement. It was often a matter of letting preconceived ideas and phrases float in a free orbit before I could direct them back through re-entry corridors to their earthing on the page. And that was a process like catching mental flies in a gravity-free zone. My temper began to flare. I was convinced in my paranoid delusions that others were stealing my thoughts. My imaginative conceptions were being transmitted through the air waves. I took to doubling on myself in the street, blanking my mind out periodically so as to resist invasion. And the cold slowed down my system of working. When you have constantly to blow on your fingers to generate heat, and to walk up and down the street in order to ensure circulation, a new rhythm

119

is imposed on the work: one of dispiritedness and despera-
tion, and something of the desire to outrage, to tear the
entrails out of the sameness and complacency of most fiction.

And despite the abolition of censorship ushered in by the
revolution, despite my sending specially bound copies of my
work to the Directory, they still pursued me. There are men
who are marked in life. No matter what they do or where
they go an indelible light burns around them. They are followed, exiled, made into examples by an impotent establish-
ment. They are like migratory deer who have been branded
while asleep, their rumps splashed with a red paintbrush. And
then it's just a matter of time. Someone will lift the jacket vent
to expose the mark, someone will snatch away the dark
glasses to reveal eyes on which is written I AM. The I in the
right pupil, the AM in the left.

I was inseparably linked to my work. The danger pursued
me. It was like a protean animal, its lowered charge would
stampede towards me in a thunder of hooves, or I would feel
the acrid reek of breath blown against my face, a leathery
tongue seeking the hollow of a cheek, the fractional divide
between my lips. And once it has found you out there's
nowhere to go. You look for yourself in the mirror and meet
with its reflection. Your feet turn into hooves in the street, a
stringy tail swings from your coccyx.

I took to staying in. These were times when a man could be
returned to his family without a head. Crazy days, when men
realized that the revolutionary principle had no need to stop.
They had made Paris into a lake of blood and had walked
across it in satin slippers. A madman had stood by the river,
calling out that this was the Red Sea. It would open for the
good if they could only see the opposite shore.

I might even have known him. Restif de la Bretonne, the
man who began to unpick the seams in my life. His mind
must have been dealing thoughts against me for months,
years. He would have listened to them build and fall at night,
an inner dialogue carrying the momentum of surf. And the
tide must have darkened, mounted in his head, the roar of
black water pushing through his veins, tipping up debris,
throwing my face up huge in his mind. He had published his

120

novel *The Anti-Justine* as a way of reproaching me publicly, of making it known that my work was by its extremity injurious to the pornographers' profession. Jealousy, embitterment, these are the black spots in the minds of men who lack breadth of vision. They entered death, I stayed in life. They extinguished their cells, while I revised my biochemistry.

On 6 March 1801 I was arrested for the seventh time in thirty-eight years. France was now under the rule of Napoleon Bonaparte as first Consul, and the people pressed towards a nationalist identity, a regeneration of authority. I was sent summarily to Sainte-Pélagie and then transferred to Bicêtre. The cell fitted itself to my spine. I had the weight of a granite cliff on my back. It felt as though the world was crushing me on two sides, yet had spared me this fissure in which to labour for breath, to lid my eyes and stare into inner space. And was it there I found my healer, the one who contributed to my being alive now? For a long time I cradled my arms and legs in a huddled centre of warmth. And then the light came on. It was white. I stared at it, transfixed, and I realized there was someone sitting in the centre. He was positioned cross-legged, his eyes closed, concentrating on an inner point. There was no connection between us other than that one had intersected with the other. But the longer I stared, the more I realized the face wasn't going to disappear. It was like looking into the sun to find the sky has vanished and left nothing but this singular, luminous punctum. When the man opened his dark-blue eyes, the power entered me. I felt the electric heat flood my veins. I vibrated with this transmission of energy. Everything that was dead in me came alive. I entered a dream. I was sitting in a metal chair, the sort of light, flexible aluminium model we use today, looking out of a studio window over Paris. A woman on the flat roof opposite was naked. A red lion lay sunning itself at her side. It got up once and drank from a bowl of water, yawned, then went back to sleep.

As a dream permits no choice, I followed the sequence of events. She was holding some sort of chart in her hands, a board on which papers rested. What I found myself looking at on the reverse of the board was the kaleidoscopic impression of DNA molecules, spiral chains viewed through an electron microscope. Of course it is only retrospect and the acquisition of biotechnological knowledge which have allowed me to interpret the dream in this way.

The woman turned her back to me and I saw the lion's head in place of her bottom, a sort of anatomically revised sphinx. Four square, black clouds stood off in the perfectly blue sky. They were like suspended building blocks. I watched them shift to the left of my vision, and awoke.

Something had happened to me. I couldn't understand the significance of these things at first. What I experienced was the expansion of inner space. There was so much room in which to be. I was no longer in a prison cell, I was anywhere. The constriction of physical space, which had so terrified me, no longer existed. I could walk across the universe and continue my journey to the stars. I had a perspective on life that no other human shared. I was totally alone. In the same way as I had written in *Juliette* that 'what I would do with the ass of my imagination, the gods themselves could not invent', so my purchase on life itself had increased to encompass possibilities which appeared to have no correlation with anyone who had ever lived.

Autumn again? If I open the car door, the smell of damp floods my senses. I close my eyes and anticipate the red and gold blaze of leaves, the patter of acorns and chestnuts: chestnuts the size of a cow's eye flipped out of their pods into the grass. Bees thud by in a crazy orbit, the wasp is drunk on apple-juice, an irascible, ciderish bullet with a jab of poison tucked into its tail. There will be a thin trail of blue smoke escaping from a bonfire at the edge of a field. Sound will carry in the still air. A voice crosses three fields as though it was confided to an ear. And what am I listening out for? A familiar voice, the beat of the universe, a stranger to approach me with news, the final news.

In the days when I considered myself mortal, I made specific requests about what was to happen to my remains after death. I shall remind you of these. The instructions were written at a time of bitterness, implicit nihilism.

I expressly forbid an autopsy. I ask that my body should be left for a period of forty-eight hours in the room I shall die in, placed in an open coffin for the duration of that time. During this interval a messenger shall be sent to Monsieur Lenormand, a wood merchant at Versailles, to ask him personally to transport my body to a wood on my property at Malmaison near Epernon, where I wish to be placed, without any sort of ceremony, in the first thicket to the right of the wood, as it is met on the main road coming from the old château. My grave shall be dug in the thicket by the Malmaison farmer under the guidance of Monsieur Lenormand, who will only leave my body after it has been buried. Relatives and friends may attend the interment, but without mourning of any kind. Once the grave has been filled it shall be sown with acorns, so that in time all trace of my tomb may disappear from the face of the earth, as I flatter myself that my memory will be erased from the minds of men, except those few whose affection for me has continued to the last.

Made at Charenton-Saint-Maurice, while of sound mind and body, 30 January 1806.

My instructions were of course mismanaged. Despite the express wish for an atheist burial, whoever it was they placed in the earth that day received Christian rites. And only days later, the phrenologist Gall sent his students to sever my head so that he could analyse the skull. But that is part of history. It hardly concerns me at all. The real issue is the fiction of identity. I am talking to you now, before the season has me resume my real life at La Coste. If there is such a thing as reincarnation, the experiential phases of life and death repeating themselves with character modifications, then almost anyone you meet or see may have been known to you in a previous life. As you grow older, so the blond-haired boy playing in the garden next door may be the father you lost years before; perhaps neither of you will ever know the truth. And your mother? Couldn't she be the attractive young woman in the tight black skirt and white blouse with a scarlet shoulder-bag who turned your head in the high street? Anything is possible once we break down the distinctions between the living and the dead.

But I simply am. My life has adjusted to the times. My investments are managed by a team of consultants; the world is made strangely small should I choose to jet-hop across its continents. My New York apartment hás a heliport. It amuses me to have my own pilot use a helicopter to bring transvestite prostitutes to me: Black, Asian, Dutch. There's a Japanese boy who makes up in the style of an ephebic geisha: a white face, black lips painted into a heart with a brush, a little film of gold dusted on his eyelids. Mostly we speak. I ask him about his clients, their particular fetishes, the spectrum he is willing to explore to appease their inclinations. And after he has gone, I write it all down:

James, a Wall Street broker. Has me visit him in a loft that is all leather. He doesn't live there. He bought it for assignations. After his mother died he developed peculiar tastes. He likes me to tie a pink satin bow round his genitals, the sort of ribbon that goes on a chocolate box. I have to lie face up on a glass table, while he positions himself beneath me on the floor. We're divided by a plane of glass. . . .

And so on. This boy, who calls himself Omi, lives out the dictates of sexual fiction. I will rewrite his narratives, they are part of that ongoing work which is my continuity. What will sex be like in the twenty-third century? Perhaps by then, it will be time for me to publish.

Omi may visit La Coste next month. I will recompense him for his time, the months of lost earnings. What I am trying to re-establish is a circle of speakers – the narrators I used in *The 120 Days of Sodom*. A company, a society, those whose task is to incite by narration. Instead of Duclos, entertaining the assembled libertines of my old novel with the scatological, necrophiliac tales of things she had experienced or witnessed, the multiplicity of perversions of which the limited

124

human anatomy is capable, I want the aural stimulus of late twentieth-century erotica.

I would invite others. Butch, whom I met in Pigalle. He'd operated for years in the Bois de Boulogne, and had been through a series of staggering physical metamorphoses. From a shaved head and a body as light as two magnetized pins, to mauve hair extensions knotted into a Rastafarian, to a Lou-Reed-*circa*-1976 image: slouch cap, black mirror glasses, red lipstick. One hand angled on a bonily obtrusive hip, Butch confronted the world with absolute defiance. She too operated through a system of private clients. The bizarre, the fetishistic, those whose needs were proscribed by society and irreconcilable with permanent relationships. Her regular clients were called Red Queen, Pink Bubble-gum, Arman the Voyeur, Jimmy Out to Lunch, Pinky the Poseur: a diary full of erotic extravaganza.

And Marleine from Amsterdam. When I met her she was flipping a fluorescent green tennis ball against a wall, smashing it and waiting for the rebound. The ball hopped frantically in and out of the light and shade. There was something about this person's resolution to sustain that rhythm which was reflected in her quality of thought. Her mind leapt from one hemisphere to the other, from the obscene to the endearingly naïve, from the sort of black humour I nurtured in my circle at La Coste, to memories of childhood, discovering a blue dash of the sky in a dewdrop, creating an imaginary lexicon from rain as it audibly scored a dry road before the downpour. Marleine had been encouraged from an early age to cross-dress, and had learnt the advantages of placing a woman's face on a man's body. It attracted the odd, individuals who belonged to a secret society, a species who lived by night in clubs, rococo bars, all gilt and mirrors, and also the rich, the more eccentric who hired her for company or assignations in their town houses or apartments.

Marleine would visit La Coste this autumn. Green eyes, partially oriental features, a silk dress slipping off an unmistakably male shoulder, the bone structure contradicting the fragility of the female gestures.

I have known so many, and each year I attempt to assemble

a new company at La Coste. Erotica is not, as some people would assume, exhaustible in its limitations and inevitable repetition, it is constantly subject to imaginative revision. The spoken word expands sexual potential. As the imagination creates new ways of seeing the world, so it likewise invents unexplored erotic possibilities. A reading of J.G. Ballard's *Crash* is just one way in which a new sexual geometry can be derived from the technology of the modern world.

These people come and go and I outlive them all. The company at La Coste is never repeated. No matter how extreme the participants are in their tastes, I am soon in need of other pleasures, other tastes. My guests arrive expecting to encounter an obese, superannuated member of the old French aristocracy, living amongst relics inherited from the past, Louis XIV escritoires, neatly bound shelves of eighteenth-century erotica, and the notorious enamelled lockets in which exaggerated postures were portrayed, or what we would call today group sex. Many of these lockets showed a woman sitting on a man's erect penis, her skirts blown around her waist, being watched by another woman, one hand beneath her skirt, the other on her friend's nipples, while a man seated behind her had inserted his hand between her legs.

But what my select visitors discover is someone vitally trim, dressed in a grey suit by Paul Smith or a black silk composition by Yves St Laurent, an orange pop-art tie spilling from a white designer shirt. My appearance confuses. Belonging to no sector of society I baffle by my inner concentration, the aura that surrounds me of someone who has never died. How does one approach such a person? However briefly we touch on people in conversation, a casual meeting across a bar counter, at a party, we're conscious of the individual death which is within them. We assess their life-enhancing qualities by the invisible degeneration apparent in their body. It's through these corresponding tensions that we take a person for human.

But Donatien-Alphonse-François de Sade? Who is this man? Inseparable from controversy, his name stamped on the covers of badly translated books written three centuries ago. And I am here in the centre of those convened at La Coste.

How many will escape with their lives? And where will they go? After the months of initial shock they will begin to speak about me. It will be in the present tense and people will mistake it for the past. They will go on doing that in order to keep me at a safe distance.

It is easier to exploit the dead; humans find security in a historic perspective without realizing that the legacy of every action gets written into their genes. Don't all dictators stand up and salute in our minds? They want to convince us that they were right. Behind the peaks of their military caps, the dead are piled up in skyscraper burial mounds. A single woman stands with her hands screening her eyes, looking for her son. He went away so long ago, leaving behind a simple farmhouse, a herd of cows in the meadow, the loose change deposited in a communal bottle by the door. He is someone with no identity, a wafer pressed between other bodies. When they were killed they hadn't eaten for two weeks. The woman places an orange rose in a jam-jar of water beside the vertical cenotaph. The train back to her village has been discontinued from lack of interest. The only way back is on foot. She will walk for three weeks down dusty roads, not a car stopping for her. This is the inheritance of the poor in the face of materialism.

I am the centre without being a part of the company. I have reached that state of unshockable invincibility whereby I am detached from the proceedings. And this is the most danger-ous condition of all. I am too deeply rooted in life, too omnivorously experienced to register shock. By the time something has reached me I have moved on, escaping always into the unknowable, the untraceable. But what goes on is of vital concern to me. I mean who fucks who, either in the imagination or the flesh. That doesn't change. Only the re-finement of thought which presides over it demands a level of expertise which few can fulfil.

Right now I have to make telephone assignations. The red leaf succeeds the orange as the yellow preceded the bronze. My diary, my address books open on cards, numbers, scarlet underlinings of black numerals. The special have been chosen from across the face of the earth, drawn from the capitals, the villages where I have sojourned in my transcontinental journeys. Who was that olive-skinned boy swinging in a hammock, a straw hat over his genitals? Later in the evening his sister crouched at his feet, the two in a conspiratorial pact to which they will give voice at La Coste. What is their relationship and how can I advance it in my singular way, make it into something which will never be forgotten? What began as the discovery of a mutual adolescent attraction will in time be translated into a union so bizarre that a vocabulary will have to be invented to describe it. And this will happen at La Coste. I shall arrive as I always do, in advance of my guests. I shall take up a chair in the huge blue library and live there with my memories. A gun will crack somewhere in the surrounding fields, a tourist bus will be making for my old ruins. They will get out, the German, French, Japanese sightseers, and think to themselves – He lived here, he must have walked across this courtyard, climbed stairs to the hollow windows. And they will try to imagine me. But giving shape to someone who fascinates them by reason of his notoriety, demands they conceive of monsters. Is a man human who leaves behind him the legacy of *The 120 Days*? Might he not have walked into this very library to set down a bowl of yellow roses? Or was he, they will ask, a prophet, someone whose unconscious involuntarily anticipated the genocidal politicians of the twentieth century? Couldn't most of my characters be translated into those world leaders who every decade threaten the existence of the planet? And aren't there Messianic connotations surrounding my name? It wasn't for nothing that Buñuel in the film *L'Age d'Or* had my creation the Duc de Blangis emerge from the winter-long orgies of *The 120 Days of Sodom* dressed as Christ. And didn't I find in Apollinaire the sympathy that brought my work to the attention of the twentieth century? And in his novel *Les Onze Mille Verges* the continuation of the work I had begun and go on doing?

If the god is present in the disease, if he is the psychic manifestation illuminating the pathological, then I have created a new pantheon. Each aberration deserves to be considered in the light of its tutelary deity. Sometimes the inner and outer exactly unite, and they are there, the many who have presided over my obsessions. But immanence is brief. A red curtain opens in the blue sky. Through a perfect rectangle I see into the back of deep space. Then the rooks are trooping over again, blackening the rainy September sky. Smoke drifts across, and pumpkins are being loaded on to a farm truck: orange, tangible suns which have been rooted in the earth, they are planets to be baked and eaten on autumn nights.

On my desk is a word-processor and a pile of books, some of which I have bought out of curiosity, because they are about me. What is it Pierre Klossowski is saying in *Sade Mon Prochain*? I will read it aloud. 'The pervert strives to execute a unique gesture; this lasts but a second. The pervert spends his existence perpetually awaiting the moment when the gesture can be executed . . . to execute this gesture corresponds in his mind to the total fact of existing.'

No one will disturb me in the library. On one wall I have hung Clovis Trouille's painting *Luxure, ou les rêveries du marquis de Sade*. In it, death and love unite with orgiastic frenzy. I am depicted whip in hand, brooding on the remains of La Coste. Voluptuous girls dressed in black stockings and high heels are constrained by bondage. My elbow rests on a skull which in turn is supported by a rose. Two goats are a part of this ritual. The girl wearing a hat has her dress split open to reveal her bottom. She lies on a flowered bank. My eyes are turned inward. What I am seeing is the idea of what I am experiencing. It's there that the real world happens.

And isn't there an innocence in the extreme nature of my experience? Behind it somewhere is my consciousness of life as a simple park with plane avenues, the benches interspersed: a secluded precinct. Three schoolgirls wearing blue macs belted at the waist are laughing over a love letter that one of them is showing to the other two. The one who holds the crumpled rectangle of white paper has auburn hair curtaining her face. The other two are dark-haired, one wears a shocking-pink lipstick. She is in love with her image and has modelled her looks on a popular singer. Her lover is a mirror. Just three schoolgirls confused by their feelings towards an adolescent met on holiday. I watched them go by. I had all the time in the world. My limousine was parked in a street running parallel to the park. In my mind, they were already naked. Tight little bottoms decorated with the lipstick obscenities I would write on their flesh, the blue crescent moons my lips would leave as a bruised imprint. I could have asserted myself, offered them tea at a nearby café, discoursed on books, art, life, gradually edging my conversation round to the theme of sexual aberration. I could have, and I did. And one of the girls returned with me, the one with the shocking-pink lipstick. She was in love with the notion of having transcended relationships. Boys could offer her nothing. She was looking for revelation, an androgyne dressed in dancer's tights and a mauve jacket studded with rhinestones, eyes blacked out, someone whose gender was an enigma. Through this person she would experience a new form of sexual union. It would be indescribable, involving a point of entry that would never have been used before. The ear? The nostril? The gaps between fingers and toes? An aperture in a secret fold of skin in the back, the side, the hip? An opening nurtured and kept alive for this confrontation with the androgyne.

I took her back to my Ile de Seine apartment. She browsed through my shelves of erotica, leafing through *The Pleasures of Cruelty, being a sequel to the reading of* Justine *and* Juliette. And, with more interest, through another curiosity, *Sadopaideia, being the experiences of Cecil Prendergast, Undergraduate of the University of Oxford: Shewing how he was led through the pleasant paths of Masochism to the supreme joys of Sadism.* Then there was Pierre Klossowski's *Le Baphomet* and several novels by André-Pieyre de Mandiargues, minor things which caught her eye, but nonetheless fuelled the curiosity which had gained such dominance within her.

I moved over to her side and took down a copy of *The 120 Days of Sodom.* I opened the book at random and, feigning surprise, read a passage aloud. 'There, everyone will meet again. . . . There, everybody will be naked: historians, wives, girls, boys, old women, fuckers, friends; everyone will be knotted together, prostrate on the flagstones, sprawling on the ground, and, after the example of animals, everyone will change, will fuck, commit incest, adultery or sodomy and, with the exception of deflowering vulvas, will indulge in

130

every excess and every form of aberration which can best excite the mind.'

Evelyn said nothing, as if she was in a trance. She unzipped her short black skirt and let it fall to her feet like a crumpled flower. She was wearing see-through panties the same shocking pink as her lipstick. She stood with her back to me looking out of the uncurtained window at the river. The light was jumping silver on green, a spine of water lit up by stars. And in that instant she was transformed into someone untouchable. Even though I lowered her panties with my teeth, bent her over an armchair, her bottom face up towards me, laid into her with my furious whip-hand, it was as though there was no one there. I could never reach the object of my passion. Evelyn was somewhere else, inviolable, contained within the chrysalis of a dream.

The value of memory. I could tell you so much, but one forgets even the most vital experiences over centuries. Today, I commit everything to the computer memory. In a century's time I shall surprise myself by learning how I lived. Meanwhile, what can I tell you of my intimate experiences? There are my letters, those which have survived, those which are still unwritten.

Paris, 19 May 1790.

A week before the siege of the Bastille, the Montreuils took the precaution of having me transferred to Charenton. There, my dear Reinaud, that aristocratic scum that goes under the name of the Montreuils, a family I despise like the filth in the streets, were despicable enough to have me vegetate for nine months in a hospital ward for madmen and epileptics. . . . I am still unable to understand how it is I did not die there. Finally, nine months later, my children came to visit me, and one of them took it into his authority to ask by what law I was detained. The jailer, not knowing the reason for my confinement, other than it was at the instigation of my wife's family, led me to the twin gates. They creaked on their hinges, and I walked free.

A moment in history. A significant hour in a man's life. And no more. History is like a continuous autumn. Whatever happens is buried under the leaf fall, and in the end it can't be retrieved. It lies too deep to be remembered. Civilizations turn to mineral, dust; epochs are written into the lexicon of subterranean strata.

My shirt is striped orange and white. Thin verticals. I wear two shirts a day, and likewise change my suit at noon. I have this fastidiousness, this need to be absolutely modern in my dress, but at the same time impeccably unostentatious. I pick up clothes when I am travelling, but more often than not my suits are made for me by the best names in Paris.

Soon, I shall hear the car draw up in the drive with the first of our autumn arrivals. Most of them will have been given a text by me which describes the happenings in the infamous Château of Silling, a topographical accident protected by a precipice. So by contrast, they will find La Coste less threatening. And once again I shall hear my transvestite assistants open the bondage cells in the château's underground maze. Pretty young men dressed in short leather skirts or hot pants will lead the way through corridors to the interior. All who come here will realize within themselves erotic impulses which were previously repressed. They will discover new erogenous zones. They will go back to the world changed. And all of them will at some stage try to return. Having entered the mythic realm of sexual initiation, having abandoned their jobs and lovers to come here, they will for ever live at a tilt to the world. The trance-like nature of their experiences will recur in dreams. It will catch them out with a longing for autumn, which is inseparable from sexual rites. Many of them will undergo sex changes, so urgent will their need be to experience pleasures observed at La Coste and exclusive to the opposite sex. In the course of my travels I encounter these persons. I drink with them in bars in Montmartre, Greenwich Village, Amsterdam, and I listen and observe. I am never recognized. They tell me the story of what I did, and it is always new to me. Was I really that one? Did I accommodate so much in my repertoire of bondage experiments? I order two more bourbons and the narrative extends its line like a spider constructing a web: silk stitches, one a truth and one a lie. My life is a continuous fabrication in every drag bar. When I'm back in the car, body moulded to the warm red leather, I take out the Walkman I have concealed on my person and listen to the conversation on cassette. And each tape becomes part of the archives from which I construct future books.

In half an hour my chauffeur will have returned from the station. Perhaps it is Omi who will be driven here. Only I won't go to greet him. He will already be different from the Omi I know, concentrated, tense, beginning the journey inwards towards self-exploration. He will spend the afternoon in the old chapel underground, meditating on the erotic frescoes, taking copious pinches of cocaine from the large crystal bowl I have placed in the room's centre. He will reappear naked. His kabuki mask will have transformed him into an initiate. Six months later he will be taken back to the station. I will see him that summer in New York, and our relationship will continue as if he had never been to the château.

In the myth or the life, call it what you will, my last days were spent in the madhouse at Charenton. It was there that I instigated the theatre that Artaud was to discover in this century. The actors were all insane. Sometimes they would set fire to the curtains, declaim with a volubility that was savagely violent, maintain a schizophrenic dialogue independent of their parts. Anything and everything became possible. Men exposed themselves on stage. Someone swallowed his script. The public audience would grow alarmed and take flight. Napoleon's ministers were informed, but the Abbé de Coulmier, who officiated over the asylum, saw a therapeutic content to drama and was able to resist the efforts of the Chief of Police to have me released from this more flexible institution and returned to prison. 'His only delirium being that of vice', so the Chief of Police argued, de Sade should be returned to the sort of fetid lair to which he had already been subjected on innumerable occasions.

The story has it that I was still sufficiently well connected to have intermediaries petition that I should be left in the unpardonable cold and mental isolation of an asylum ward rather than endure the harrowing containment of a cell.

The plays were discontinued after culminating in an outrage of public indecency. A donkey on stage involuntarily produced an erection, excited as it was by the stimulus of human sweat and body scents released by a red-haired actress. Several times in the course of the play she had scissored her legs open beneath her skirts to reveal that she was wearing crotchless panties. When the donkey made a run at her, the audience invaded the stage. It was a piece of unintentional Sadeian humour which led to the termination of all theatre in the asylum. A century later, this might have happened at the Cabaret Voltaire and been applauded.

Today, I am full of memories. They build up like cumulus and as soon disperse. What is important is that the individual should always oppose the collective; the spirit of revolution in the arts, in political ideologies, must be paramount if our civilization is not to die at the hands of celluloid cut-outs, men whose separation from their inner lives has become so total that they are the first race of Externals.

I shall outlive you all. I am preparing myself for that final solitude. I shall not be totally alone, for the best of my transvestite assistants have also been programmed by me to function without cellular decay. I will spare Omi, Butch and Marleine, and I shall find Philippe. They will remain with me after the human species has migrated towards extinction. Imagine it, the inheritors of the ruined earth will be transvestites, transsexuals, those who have opposed their chromosomal gender.

The car returns with greater regularity. I notice from my window that a blonde girl with green eyes and her chestnut-haired friend are running to retrieve a loose page which has slipped free from a pocket book, a diary. And will I find Evelyn arrived one rainy afternoon when the big yellow plane leaves splash down on the drive? She will still be wearing her raincoat belted at the waist, her shocking-pink lipstick, her shocking-pink panties. She will go to the chapel and pray that this time she is taken in the flesh.

What I have created remains. What anyone relates of a life is a fragment, a piece of glass broken free of the crystal, a micro-chip displaced from its system. The leaves are flying. The vine is weighted to breaking point. *The 120 Days of Sodom* was written between 22 October and 28 November 1785 in the Bastille. Its reverberations continue to trouble the world, but it is a small thing compared to what I have prepared for the future. The sexual ethos I envisaged has been enacted to the last token. Who reading this has not subscribed to at least one of my polysexual recommendations?

The room is always waiting. Its walls are black leather, the bed is black satin. A horned minotaur gets up lazily from a red rug and shambles out of the room. The video circuit comes alive. The silence is so charged that it vibrates with the energy preceding a storm. I can hear my footsteps echoing ten paces behind the staccato click of high heels. We seem to have been walking for centuries underground. I don't know whether it's a man or woman whom I follow. Occasionally solitary clouds blow down the corridor. They are like pieces of a dream, vaporous mosaics burning over into the deserts inhabited by Dali and Tanguy, the great spaces of the imagination. A street scene dominated by fire and by hordes of crazy looters whizzes over my right shoulder, its impact lighter than a snowflake. Events in the oneiric cosmos arrive as hallucinatory flashbacks. We keep on walking, always divided by the same distance. Her heels leading, mine in pursuit. There is no hurry; our orgasm when it arrives will last for a thousand years. I will flip her on to her stomach and enter by way of a constriction that is excruciatingly timeless. The world goes by in the opposite direction.

And aren't we walking directly into the future I have apprehended? The figure in front of me wears nothing but a gold tanga brief. At some stage I will lift the narrow triangle at the back and disappear. I have the impression I will be making love in deep trance, attempting like an astronaut to connect in a gravity-free zone. The heels continue clicking. The ceiling lights are spaced at regular intervals. This time we are on a long voyage. My bodyguards follow me. The lords of the underworld acknowledge our passing. Roses and excrement. Small animals, startled by our footsteps, jump to one side. There's no choice but to go on. I think it's Omi who walks in front of me but it could be anyone. Together we will achieve a new race. I shall tell you my name a last time. Donatien-Alphonse-François de Sade. Let the future proclaim it. The heels again. Panthers slink tamely past in the opposite direction, prowling from cell to cell. A cobra lies across our path, its somnolent skin like a rain sky reflected in a cloudy lagoon. There are lions, sprawling leopards, tigers, the menagerie I keep underground. Castrati sing in the eroticized chapel. We are the untouchables. We are exempt from the heat-flash, the universal catastrophe. A woman in black leather thigh boots emerges from a room carrying a spear-shaped red feather. Her female lover waits on her haunches in the cell opposite. A sphinx crawls out of a dream and breaks up into sand that dusts our feet. We are on a journey to the centre of inner space. The archetypes undergo their continuous metamorphoses, they are the pathways in the unconscious kingdom. My clothes fall away from me and are gathered by my attendant. My penis breaks into flower, an orgiastic efflorescence of purple and white. My direction is assured. Huge birds flap by on leather wings. And still the heels click in front of me. It's not very far. Our union will be the evolution of a myth. The child will be taken back to the earth and driven away in a closed car. Its mother will be the first transvestite to have given birth. This child will stand saluting on a white beach as the world ends. As for us, the pleasure is still anticipated. The primal orgasm which seeded the stars is re-enacted each year at La Coste. Only we invert it.

I have the feeling I am narrowing in on my partner. He lets his gold tanga snap loose from two clips at the sides. Way above us, the gold leaves will be falling too, over the turrets, the drives, over the few we have elected to join us at La Coste.

PETER OWEN

A PETER OWEN PAPERBACK